Jake,
reinvented

ALSO BY GORDON KORMAN

Son of the Mob

Son of the Mob 2: Hollywood Hustle

Maxx Comedy

I Want to Go Home

The Macdonald Hall series

The Everest trilogy

The Island trilogy

The Dive trilogy

Jake,
reinvented

GORDON KORMAN

Scholastic Canada Ltd.

Toronto New York London Auckland Sydney
Mexico City New Delhi Hong Kong Buenos Aires

Scholastic Canada Ltd.

175 Hillmount Road, Markham, Ontario L6C 1Z7, Canada

Scholastic Inc.

555 Broadway, New York, NY 10012, USA

Scholastic Australia Pty Limited

PO Box 579, Gosford, NSW 2250, Australia

Scholastic New Zealand Limited

Private Bag 94407, Greenmount, Auckland, New Zealand

Scholastic Ltd.

Villiers House, Clarendon Avenue, Leamington Spa,
Warwickshire CV32 5PR, UK

Library and Archives Canada Cataloguing in Publication

Korman, Gordon

Jake, reinvented / Gordon Korman.

ISBN 0-439-96933-6 (bound).—ISBN 0-439-95789-3 (pbk.)

I. Title.

PS8571.O78J35 2003   jC813'.54   C2003-904042-9

6 5 4 3 2 1   Printed in Canada   05 06 07 08

For Jay and Daisy

$\mathcal{H}$e had come a long way to this blue lawn, and his dream must have seemed so close that he could hardly fail to grasp it. He did not know that it was already behind him. . . .

—F. Scott Fitzgerald, *The Great Gatsby*

chapter
one

ON A SCALE OF one to ten, this party was at least an eight. It was in full swing by the time we crashed it. Not that you can ever crash when you're with Todd Buckley. Todd's invited everywhere, and he brings who he pleases. Quarterback's privilege.

The carpet smelled like beer already, so I knew the festivities had been going on for a while. The stereo must have set somebody back a few bucks, because when the bass was cranked, you could feel the air move. The floor was moving too, under the stomping feet of a mob of dancers. Arms and legs jostled the shiny keg, which sat in a little kids' inflatable wading pool by the living room–dining room.

As we watched, Nelson Jaworski staggered in from the hall and hit the wading pool face-first in a tidal wave of ice and slush. There was a roar of laughter until the big lineman sprang back to his feet, snatched up the keg like it weighed nothing, and reared back to heave it through the picture window.

Todd and I joined the stampede to stop him.

"Take it easy, buddy," Todd soothed. "If you trash the keg, it means we're out of beer."

The logic was fairly straightforward, but what got through to Nelson was the fact that it was coming from Todd. "Yeah, yeah, I'm cool, I'm cool."

By that time, somebody had the brains to wave a full cup under his nose. He surrendered the keg into the arms of the three guys it took to set it back in the pool.

Todd was laughing as we pushed through the crowd. "What do you think, Rick? This is what you've been missing."

I worked as a camp counselor in the summer, so I skipped the first two weeks of football practice that our team always had before the start of school. I was a little out of the loop. "This guy Jake—he moved here while I was away?"

Todd smirked. "Coach thinks he dropped straight from heaven. He's a long-snapper. That's all he does."

"No way!" Coach Hammer didn't let anyone get away with doing only one job. Even Todd, his precious superstar, played nickel back and anchored the onside kick coverage team.

"No bull," Todd assured me. "Coach got sick of watching Nelson heave the ball twenty feet over your head, and now he's got a guy who does nothing but snap long. I'll introduce you."

I was the kicker and backup QB. Second fiddle to Todd. Story of my life.

Since I was with him, I was in on the endless procession of high-fives and backslaps that our quarterback seemed to draw like a magnet as we toured the party.

Everybody was there—most of the football team, their girlfriends, the cheerleaders, and a bunch of their boyfriends and friends, the cooler people from student council, and a collection of athletes from basketball and track. I noticed some sophomore girls whose names I didn't know—they'd really filled out over the summer—and a few guys who played in their own rock band. It was the guest list that really made this bash what it was. If I could put together the party of my dreams—not that my parents ever left me alone in the house for more than five minutes—this was exactly the kind of crowd I'd want. I marveled at how a newcomer like Jake Garrett could waltz into town and instantly know all the right people to invite.

I turned to Todd. "Do you see him?"

Todd shook his head. "Must be upstairs."

"Don't his parents notice that there are fifty kids going nuts in their house?" I asked.

"Jake's dad's out of town five days a week," Todd explained. "His mom lives in Texas somewhere." He picked up a slice of pizza from a table that was loaded with the stuff, folded it expertly, and took a bite. "Last week," he mumbled, "I dared Nelson to do ten beers and ten slices in ten minutes. Puked his guts out from Mr. Garrett's bedroom window. Killed a rosebush."

I had to laugh. As quarterback and kicker, Todd and I entrusted our lives to Nelson on the football field. And he delivered. But off the field, it would take two of that guy to make a half-wit. Right now we could see him totally passed out on the living room couch. Someone had stuck a plastic daffodil up his nose. They never would have tried it if he had been awake.

I nudged Todd, but his attention was definitely

elsewhere. He was having a little nonverbal communication with one of the sophomore girls. This was the real reason Todd loved these parties. It had nothing to do with who barf-bombed a rosebush. The ladies loved Todd, but not half as much as he loved them. Never mind that Todd had been going out with Didi Ray for over a year now. On a scale of one to ten, Didi was a twelve on a bad day. This sophomore was in the low sevens, tops. But the sophomore was here, and Didi was not. And mostly, Todd was Todd.

They began to close the distance between them, moving in that trancelike state that is so dramatic and all phony. It would have been a really romantic moment except for the three guys standing on their heads against the wall trying to chug upside down while a cheering section bellowed encouragement. I think they were betting on the outcome. My money was on more dead rosebushes.

Just when Todd was a few feet away from his quarry, a hand with painted red fingernails grabbed him by the collar and yanked him to one side. It was cheerleader Melissa Fantino, who was no more than a six. But certain parts of her were pretty much off the scale. She dragged Todd into the bathroom, then slammed and locked the door behind them.

I was amazed. Melissa was Nelson's girl-friend. Messing with her was like gargling nitro.

I waited for the bathroom door to open. This was a joke, right? Those two would come giggling out, busting my chops for being so gullible as to believe that something was really happening in there.

The door stayed shut. I sure hoped Todd knew what he was doing.

With the only main-floor bathroom out of service indefinitely, I headed upstairs in search of facilities. On the way, I passed two sleepers—one on the landing, and one draped across the top step. The second guy had a couple of friends with him, if you could call them that. They were laughing like maniacs while empty-ing a squeeze bottle of contact-lens solution into the poor kid's open mouth.

When I finally climbed over that obstacle, I had to revise my estimate of the attendance at this party. There were about twenty people packed into the hall alone. But while downstairs was wild and crazy, the second floor seemed to be the designated chill-out area. The range of conversations was amazing—everything from baseball to the meaning of life. A bunch of guys from the JV football team were reciting the first Austin Powers movie line by line. I can't imagine how the subject came up, but there was a group debating the merits of Canadian bacon versus regular ham for breakfast. The Canadian-bacon advocate was so impassioned that he looked like he was ready to start throwing punches if the argument didn't go his way.

I found what I thought was a bathroom door and threw it open. There was a high-pitched female scream, followed by an angry male voice: "Get out of here, man!"

Quickly, I retreated. I didn't know who the girl was, but the voice belonged to our full-back—after Nelson, the toughest kid on the team.

"Each year, the young salmon swim up-stream, fighting the current, to spawn," came a deadpan voice behind me.

I wheeled. There, his face buried in an enor-mous bag of jalapeño-and-pineapple pretzels, sat Dipsy.

To this day I couldn't tell you his real name. We called him Dipsy—after the Teletubby, the green one with the phallic symbol growing out of his head—because he had a cowlick that stood straight up at attention. He said stuff like that all the time. You could never quite tell if he was serious, or if it came from whatever he was smoking. Although, to be honest, I never saw Dipsy smoking anything. It was just the simplest explanation for his weird personality and his perpetual munchies.

"Where's the bathroom?"

"Occupied," came the reply from the pretzels. His languid gaze traveled down the hallway of closed doors. "Everything's occupied. Except—"

Without standing, turning, or missing a bite, he reached over his shoulder and tried the knob behind him. Locked. The brass was shiny and unscuffed—obviously new. And there was a keyhole—it was made for a front door, not a bedroom.

"Our host likes his privacy," I commented.

"The great white shark is a solitary hunter, its isolation ensured by row upon row of razor-sharp teeth."

"You've got to get the cable company to take Animal Planet off your TV," I advised, adding, "Is Jake a friend of yours?"

He shrugged. "Are you a friend of mine?"

In fact, the bizarre remark almost made sense. In a way, Dipsy was everybody's friend and nobody's at the same time. He was kind of the misfit on the guest list since he wasn't really popular, or on any team or club or anything like that. Yet he was always there, shoulder to shoulder with the jocks and cheerleaders, with his ripped-up jean jacket and his inventory of junk food. He never seemed to mind the players cracking on him, which they did mercilessly. One time at the mall, a whole bunch of them lifted up Dipsy's rusty Fiat and turned it sideways in its parking spot, locked in by two other cars. The poor guy had to wait three hours for the people on either side of him to leave. But he never complained, and he always came back. And nobody tried to keep him away, which was more than you could say for the way Todd and his crowd treated a lot of other kids.

"Of course I'm a friend of yours."

"Yeah?" He regarded me expectantly.

I guess I was supposed to present my résumé to prove it. The truth was that, while I'd grown up with Dipsy, I didn't know him very well. Part of that was Dipsy's fault. He wasn't exactly Mr. Communication—except maybe to Jacques Cousteau.

I definitely wasn't his enemy. I didn't pick on him like the other Broncos. Once, back when we were sophomores, Dipsy really came through for me in a tough spot. Maybe I should have shown my gratitude a little more over the years. But Dipsy didn't seem to care. He was always too busy talking about manta rays.

"You've got a million friends," I said finally. "We just can't find you hiding upstairs in a bag of pretzels."

He replied, "The remora bides its time on the coral reef, waiting for . . ."

I didn't stick around for the rest of it. Partly because I wasn't in the mood for *Waterworld*, but mostly because the bathroom opened up.

I had to run to beat out one of the *Austin Powers* cast. While I was washing up, there was an eruption of high-pitched screaming from the yard. I peered through the curtains. In the back, some football players had turned the hose on a couple of those sophomore girls.

I raced down the stairs and outside. I think kickers are natural team peacemakers, since coaches always send us in from the sidelines to intervene when the shoving starts. But when I got to the main floor, the two would-be fire-fighters—receivers on our team—had turned suddenly chivalrous. One was wrapping the waterlogged girls in throw blankets from the couch, while the other got them drinks. The keg was pretty low by this time, so while our tight end poured, this kid I didn't know pumped the handle on top to keep the beer coming.

I turned to the shivering girls. "You'll have to excuse my friends. They get a little carried away at parties."

I don't think they even noticed I was there. They were the center of attention, and they couldn't have been any happier about that. The kid at the keg poured himself a cup and then one for me too. "Here you go, baby."

I personally think beer tastes like sand, but I accepted the drink. The music was too loud to go into a long explanation, especially to a stranger. I checked out the newcomer. He looked like he'd just waltzed off the pages of the J. Crew catalog, or maybe Banana Republic. I mean, nothing he was wearing was all that special—just a plaid shirt, untucked, over a white tee and khakis. But everything went together perfectly, and hung on him with that rumpled casual effect that you can't get by being casual. This guy **worked** at it.

We were kind of the odd men out, since there was definitely a love connection in the works between the receivers and the soggy sophomores.

I guess he saw me eyeing my beer with distaste. "There's more to drink in the laundry room, baby," he told me. "Booze, wine, soda. The washing machine's packed with ice."

I was impressed. "This guy Jake throws quite a party."

At first he looked as if he didn't understand. Then he said, "I'm Jake."

"Oh, sorry!" Feeling stupid, I fumbled to shake his hand. "I'm Rick Paradis."

"Rick the kicker!" he exclaimed. "I'm your new long-snapper, baby. We're going to be working together on the Broncos!"

An arm appeared around each of our shoulders. "I see you guys are getting to know each other."

It was Todd, looking pretty disheveled after his interlude in the bathroom. Melissa, his partner in wrinkles and lipstick smears, was in the dining room with some other cheerleaders, sending burning glances in his direction.

"*A-choo!*" On the couch, Nelson sneezed the daffodil out of his nostril and shook himself awake.

In one quick motion, I tossed my drink in Todd's face and wiped the lipstick off his mouth with my hand. Nelson was pretty wrecked. But only one girl at this party was wearing lipstick the color of stale doggy-doo. He wouldn't have to be Einstein to put it all together.

"What are you, crazy, Rick?" Todd sputtered.

Nelson took one look at us and lapsed back into his coma.

I didn't know how much I could say in front of Jake, so I just muttered, "You've got to watch out for yourself, man."

Jake gave us a knowing smile, like this was some juicy conspiracy that only the three of us were in on. "The word is you've got the hottest girlfriend in town," he told Todd. "Rumor?"

"Didi's the real deal," I supplied.

"You should have brought her," Jake told Todd.

Our quarterback shrugged. "I can have Didi any time I want. Tonight's all about . . ." He let his eyes wander appreciatively around the room. "You sure give great parties, man!"

Jake turned to me. "How about you, baby? Got a girlfriend?"

I shook my head. "No."

"Because he's an idiot," Todd finished for me. "Didi's best friend, Jennifer—goes to school with Didi at St. Mary's—she *loves* this guy! Guess who wants to be just friends."

"Nothing wrong with that," put in Jake.

Todd rolled his eyes. "Listen, Didi and Jennifer are more than inseparable. They're like Siamese twins. Half the time, when I go out with Didi, I'm stuck with Jennifer too."

"So I have to date Jennifer to make you happy," I finished for him. "There's a great basis for a relationship."

"Basis, shmasis," Todd scoffed. "Jen's hot."

And she was. But not for me. Us being just friends—that was Jennifer's decision, not mine. Todd knew that better than anybody. He was the one who'd personally sealed the deal.

At that moment, a great laughing cheer went up in the house. I wheeled just in time to see Dipsy, in his underwear, running down the stairs in pursuit of three football players who had his pants. The crowd parted to make room for the thieves, who raised their catch over their heads like Olympic gold medalists running with the flag. Bellowing trumpet sounds, they tossed the Levi's up onto one of the blades of the living-room ceiling fan. Round and round went the jeans, legs dangling.

Dipsy made a couple of jumps at the fan, but Michael Jordan he wasn't. He disappeared into the kitchen and came back with a chair, all the while ignoring the dozens of people who were slapping and pinching his butt. When he finally got up there, someone cranked the fan to maximum speed. He made a couple of snatches, but his pants were whipping by so fast, he couldn't get the timing right. At last, he grabbed hold of a leg, overbalanced and fell into a pack of cheerleaders. Amazingly, they caught him—they practiced catching Melissa for their regular routine. But he was a lot heavier than she was, and the whole group keeled over under his weight. One girl conked her head on the edge of the pizza table, and her basketball boyfriend got mad and went after Dipsy. The poor guy was hopping around, trying to get his jeans back on, while staying ahead of six-foot-three inches of outraged muscle. Plants got knocked over. Pizza slid off the table and onto the floor. Drinks were spilling left, right, and center as the pursuer and the pursued bumped and jostled everybody.

Todd slapped me on the back. "It's going to be a great senior year!"

Jake was watching the goings on with unruffled calm. Like it didn't bother him in the slightest that his house was getting trashed. Very cool under fire, this new kid.

On a scale of one to ten, I bumped the party up to a nine.

chapter
two

"**Hᴜᴛ-ʜᴜᴛ!**"

The snap was like a cruise missile, guided by telemetry right into my hands. I was so used to having to scramble for it, or at least jump, that I dropped the ball. I scooped it up on the first bounce, bobbled it briefly and kicked with all my might.

The punt was nearly vertical, bending slightly as it reached its apex. Then it plummeted into a pack of offensive linemen.

"Heads!" I called.

They scattered.

"Good hang-time, baby!" called Jake, grinning.

Todd jogged over and put his arm around my shoulders. "Senior year, Rick. You only get one."

He gestured over to where Nelson was sucker-punching the tackling dummy. "Unless you're Jaworski. You've got to play to the front row."

I tried to follow his gaze. His eyes were focused on the empty bleachers of F. Scott Fitzgerald High's third-rate football field.

I didn't get it. "Who's in the front row?"

He looked at me as if I had a cabbage for a head. "Scouts. College scouts." I guess I seemed pretty bewildered because he added, "They're not here now, but they will be!"

"What college is going to send their scouts to a dump like Fitz?" I asked.

Todd chuckled. "Come on, Rick. I'm good, but I'm not *that* good. They're going to want to see me play before they offer a big scholarship. And while they're scouting me, that's the golden opportunity for the rest of you to get noticed!"

Jake gave me another perfect snap, and this time I got off a fairly decent punt—at least this one went forward.

Was Todd serious? College scouts? I mean, he was pretty good for around here. But I couldn't picture Miami or Notre Dame so desperate for talent that they'd send their people to Fitz. That would be scraping the bottom of the barrel. Everybody knew that.

Even Coach Hammer knew it. Of course, that didn't stop him from making his usual inspirational speech at practice on the first day of school. He babbled on about the great tradition of "the old green-and-gold," which we players secretly called "the old snot-and-mustard." Naturally, no one reminded the coach that last year the Broncos had gone six and eight in a league where even the champions were pretty mediocre. And for sure nobody mentioned that the great tradition consisted of citations for ineligible players, steroid use, vandalism, and a former coach who was presently doing time for grand theft auto.

"So it's up to us to carry the banner of that legacy in the new millennium," the coach finished. I wondered if he was willing to do his part by boosting a Corvette like the old coach.

He clapped his hands. "All right—ten laps and hit the showers!"

As we headed for the cinder track that ringed the field, he pulled me aside. "Not you, Paradis. We're going to have a little talk about field goals."

I popped off my helmet and walked to the sidelines with him. "What's up, Coach?"

He draped a beefy arm around my shoulder

pads. "I'm not stupid. I heard the guys snicker when I talked about last season. But we lost four of those games by three points or less. And let's face it—at least once a game we blew a field goal because of a bad snap."

I could see where he was going with this. "Jake's great, Coach. He's practically automatic."

He nearly put his finger through my chest protector. "You have to be automatic too, Rick. From thirty yards or less. You can be the difference between six and eight and making the playoffs. Starting tomorrow, Jake, Todd, and you—the snap, the hold, the kick. Thirty minutes."

"Got it." I couldn't help asking, "What else does Jake do on the field? Besides snap, I mean."

"That's it," the coach replied. "That's his job. Long-snapper."

I was confused. "But you always said that quarterbacks should tackle, receivers should punt, and linemen should learn to throw. Don't you remember? You said if you want to be a specialist, go to proctology school."

"This guy's different," Coach Hammer tried to explain. "He's not a football player. He's too slow, he's not strong enough, and he can't throw. He can't even pick up the ball with one hand. He's got no skills."

"So what made you recruit him?" I asked, mystified.

"I didn't," the coach shrugged. "He recruited himself. Last June, after school is out, I'm in my office winding up the year, and he just kind of shows up. Says he's moving to the district and he wants to play for the Broncos. So I ask him the usual questions—what experience he's had, what positions he's played. Zero. He doesn't know football from Go Fish. But he's begging me—won't take no for an answer. So finally, just to get him out of the office, I say, 'I need a long-snapper. If you can be a long-snapper, you can play on my team.' I figured I'd never see the kid again. But there he was, sitting on the floor outside my office when I went to open it up in August. And he was a long-snapper—a good one!"

I frowned. It was possible. Long-snapping wasn't brain surgery. But why would anybody bother? I mean, it's nice to be on a football team if you're a football player. But if you're not, what's the point of finding some obscure way to sneak in through the side door? It seemed like a lot of sweat for nothing.

I looked over at the track. There was Jake, way out in front of the pack. Then I realized that he was really last, and the rest of the guys were lapping him. It was a big switch from the image of the confident, universally loved host at the party Friday night.

I stuck around and practiced kickoffs for another half-hour. So I was all by myself in the locker room when I showered up to go home. Since it was too late for the school bus, I headed for the nearest transit stop. The local bus service was pretty pathetic—students called it "the disoriented express." I settled in for a long wait.

A well-modulated horn brought me out of my public-transit coma. A champagne-colored BMW with a twenty-four-karat shine whispered up to the curb in front of me. Soundlessly, the tinted window of the driver's seat disappeared into the door. There at the wheel sat none other than Jake Garrett.

"Hey, baby, need a ride?"

I swear, I wish I could have had my clothes dry-cleaned before depositing myself into the leather interior.

"This your car, Jake?"

"Sort of," he replied.

"Sort of?"

"My dad got it after the divorce," he explained. "So since it replaced my mother, it's sort of my car. Anyway, he's never around to drive it."

"I live just down the block from you," I told him. "I can walk it from your place."

"Uh-huh." He acted as if he hadn't heard. He pulled up at a stoplight and turned to me suddenly. "Listen, baby, are you in a hurry to get home?"

I shrugged. "Not really. Why?"

"I need to pick up something," he told me. "It's for a little get-together I'm planning for this Friday."

I laughed. "I've seen your 'little get-togethers.' There's nothing little about them. There were kids at school today still feeling the effects of last Friday."

If he thought that was funny, he didn't let on. "This won't take long. Could you give me a hand?"

It just goes to show what a little luxury will do to you. I was grooving on the smooth ride and the soft leather and the CD player. By the time I paid any attention to our whereabouts, we were on the expressway halfway downtown.

"Hey, where are we going?"

"To college."

I thought he was joking. But ten minutes

later we were pulling up to the main gate of the Atlantica University campus.

"I'm visiting my brother," Jake told the guard. "He lives in Throckmorton Hall."

As we drove through, I asked, "How old's your brother?"

He grinned. "I'm an only child, baby."

I was blown away—not that he lied, but that he was such a natural at it.

We snaked along the tree-lined maze of roads that led to offices, labs, classroom buildings, and dormitories. When you're a high-school senior, you tend to think of yourself as the very top of the pyramid. Looking at the college kids changed my mind about that. We were big shots now, but only a year away from being dogmeat again.

Throckmorton Hall was a huge stone structure that had seen better days. There was a wide driveway in front, but Jake pulled up at the rear, in a narrow alley behind a very ripe garbage Dumpster. He popped the trunk.

I don't know what I expected to find in there, but I was equal parts disappointed and relieved when all I saw was the empty keg from last Friday's party.

This was my first time in a college dorm, so

I was nervous that a couple of high-school kids would get kicked out. But when you're carrying a keg, you just kind of fit in. Anyway, Jake Garrett seemed to be just as popular here as he was with the kids at Fitz. Halfway up the stairs, this beautiful girl threw her arms around him and cried, "Jake, you saved my life! I love you!"

Guys were slapping him on the back, ruffling his hair, and treating him like he owned the place.

At room 306, I met Marty Rapaport, who was Jake's keg connection. Marty, who looked like a pudgy Jerry Seinfeld, was in his last year of pre-dent. He made a big show of checking my teeth. He'll never know how close he came to getting his fat finger bitten off.

"That cross-bite should have been taken care of years ago," he clucked disapprovingly.

"Good meeting you too," I mumbled when I had my mouth back.

Then came the business of the day. There was quite a lot of it. We exchanged our empty keg for a shiny full new one. Jake had a little white envelope for Marty, and two thick manila envelopes for these other guys who came by. In return, those two handed small white envelopes to Jake. It was all very friendly, but really pretty secretive. For sure I was the only one who didn't understand exactly what was going on.

Marty caught me following the parade of envelopes. "Inquiring minds want to know," he commented.

I was embarrassed. Here was Jake, trusting me enough to bring me along to this meeting, and I was gawking like a ten-year-old at his first *Playboy*.

But Jake just said, "Don't worry about Rick, baby. He's cool."

So I did my best to fit into the Throckmorton scene. This consisted primarily of acting bored and inserting random curse words into every ordinary sentence. I tried not to be impressed by the college girls who came by to say hi to Jake. For some reason, they all wanted to talk about their *grades*. "I got an A-minus;" "I got a B-plus." Mostly, I didn't ask what was in those little envelopes. I was pretty sure it had to be money.

Lifting the full keg was a major operation. As we struggled down the back steps, I managed to pant, "I thought you were smarter than this, Jake. If you were going to bring one of the guys, it should have been Nelson."

He laughed. "At least I can rely on you not to

drink it all before we get halfway home. The party wouldn't be much of a success with an empty keg."

I asked the million-dollar question: "Does the guy doing the heavy lifting at least get an invitation?"

Jake looked surprised. "Of course. In fact, if you know any cool people you want to bring along, go for it."

That kind of caught me off guard. The way the kids at school looked at Jake these days, he was practically the Picasso of parties. I assumed he wanted to be in charge of every brush stroke.

"I don't know, Jake," I began. "You've got a pretty good thing going. Maybe the guest list should be up to you."

We had reached the alley behind the dorm. Fumbling with his left hand, Jake dug the keyless remote out of his pocket and popped the trunk of the Beamer.

"I trust you, baby," he told me, flashing me a look that I was beginning to call the Jake smile. I'm not sure I can totally describe it. At least half of it was paternalistic, like he was a really cool uncle you loved hanging out with. But the other half was pure mischievous fifth-grader—he was the kid you'd partner with to stink-bomb the teachers' lounge. It was an unbeatable combination because it appealed to your responsible and rebellious sides at the same time.

"Anyway," he went on, "a party needs fresh blood. If it's always the same people it gets boring." We dropped the keg into the trunk and closed the lid.

"I'll let you know if I think of anybody," I told him.

But he wasn't willing to drop the subject yet. "How about that girl Todd was talking about? The one who likes you?"

"You mean Jennifer? She's not from Fitz. She goes to St. Mary's with Todd's girlfriend."

"That's exactly what I'm talking about," he said as we got in the car and started for home. "Fresh blood."

The return trip took a lot longer. It was rush hour by that time. Finally, we pulled up in front of Jake's house and began the task of hauling that ninety-ton keg out of the trunk.

"Richard Paradis," came a disapproving voice from the other side of the Garretts' cedar hedge. "I never thought I'd see you falling in with a bad crowd!"

I almost groaned out loud, and Jake rolled his eyes. Every community has a town crab. Ours was Mrs. Appleford, who I just realized was Jake's next-door neighbor. My folks were friendly with her for the same reason everybody else was—they were scared to death of her. Mrs. Appleford had the complaint line for every town agency programmed on her speed-dial. If you got on her bad side, it was only a matter of time before she caught you putting out your garbage five minutes early, and ratted you out to the authorities.

"Hi, Mrs. Appleford," I called. "How are you?"

"Very disappointed," she replied. Everything disappointed Mrs. Appleford. If she ever said something positive about anyone at all, a whole lot of people in this neighborhood would keel over dead from the shock. "I never thought I'd see a nice boy like you involved in underage drinking."

"Underage drinking?" I guess it was because I didn't really drink much myself that I was able to forget I was standing in front of her with a keg on my shoulder.

Jake spoke up, smooth as always. "The beer's for my dad, ma'am. He does a lot of entertaining for business." He sounded so sincere I almost believed it myself.

Mrs. Appleford wasn't buying it. "I've been around this earth long enough to be able to spot a phony, young man. And I'm looking at one right now. I think the police would be very interested to know what goes on at your home when your father's away." And she stormed off into her house and slammed the door.

"She'll do it, you know," I moaned. "She'll call the police, the FBI, Interpol, and maybe even God."

Jake was impressed. "I didn't think she could even see as far as my place through those Coke-bottle glasses. She doesn't miss much."

"She doesn't miss *anything*," I assured him. "She could probably quote your driver's license number to the cops when she turns you in."

"I'm not going to let a nosy neighbor stop me." It was odd the way he said it—like he was talking about a sacred quest. A high-school bash as the Holy Grail.

We rolled the keg into Jake's garage—he wouldn't have to start chilling it until the night before the party.

I headed for the door. "I'll see you at practice tomorrow."

"Thanks for your help," he called after me. "Let me know what Jennifer says about the party."

I stopped in my tracks. For a guy who played his whole life just about as cool as anybody I'd ever met, he sure seemed pretty hung up on this one thing.

"Okay," I agreed. "I'll give her a call."

"Only if you want," he replied airily. "It's totally up to you, baby."

chapter
three

JENNIFER BELANGER KNEW how to dress for a
party. She was an athlete—soccer, track, tennis,
you name it—so the miniskirt was her weapon
of choice. Another inch off that hem and she
could have kissed the PG-13 rating good-bye.

Jennifer and I had known each other our
whole lives. Our folks were best friends. When
we were really little, we used to take baths
together on vacations. The mere thought of that
happening today could brown out my concentration for weeks. It was an exercise in visuali-
zation that I practiced far more often than I
cared to admit.

She liked me—there was no question about
that. But painful experience had taught me it

was a brother–sister kind of like, nothing more. I was her buddy, her confidant, with a Just Friends visa indelibly stamped in my passport to Jennifer. And in that area anyway, life sucked.

"Ricky—hi!" She twirled in front of me, highlighting her outfit. "What do you think? Donna Karan."

"She loaned you the dress?"

She laughed in my face. "Donna Karan the designer, stupid! Jeez, Ricky! I thought you were a kicker! You've got the brains of a nose tackle."

"The guys'll be drooling over you." I had firsthand info. "Ready to go?"

"Sure," she said. "Didi should be here any minute."

Uh-oh. "Didi's coming?"

She turned those brown eyes on me. "You don't mind, do you, Ricky? Todd blew her off again. He has some family thing to go to."

Gee, I thought sarcastically. I never knew Todd Buckley and Jake Garrett were related. Aloud I stammered, "I—I gotta use your phone."

Well, I had to at least give Todd the heads-up that Didi was going to be at the party. Not that I cared whether or not Todd got busted. But if he decided to blame me for it, he could make things pretty difficult for me around school and on the Broncos.

The phone rang and rang. Todd had already left.

I toyed with the idea of telling the girls the party had been canceled. But then I'd end up missing out on a really great night. It boiled down to this: Was I placed on this earth for the sole purpose of making life easier for Todd Buckley?

I went back out onto the porch. "Okay, let's saddle up—" My voice trailed off.

Didi had arrived. It made no sense that my first sight of her should always render me deaf and dumb. I mean, she was awesome, but I knew that already. Maybe what dazzled me was how *flawless* she was. There were a lot of good-looking people out there who still had funny noses or weird hair or the occasional zit. But Didi was pure magazine cover, airbrushed to perfection—from the big stuff, like a face that would stop traffic, right on down to the delicate curl of every single eyelash.

I didn't have a crush on her—no more than every other male on the planet, anyway. But you have to have a certain amount of respect for something so spectacular, whether it's the Grand Canyon or a girl.

"Hi, Didi. How's it going?"

She drew in a sharp, impatient breath. "You don't want to know." That was classic Didi. She wasn't being rude; she was just answering my question. It was like meeting a hotshot executive who truly can't spare the mental energy to think about you very much. Of course, Didi had never held so much as a paper route in her entire life.

To hang out with Jennifer and Didi was to learn what it is to be ignored. How two people who lived right next door to each other, went to school together, and spent most of their waking hours in each other's company still had so much to discuss was beyond me.

They talked about guys like I wasn't even there—who was cute, and who had a great butt, and who used to have nice pecs until his father sold the weight set, blah, blah, blah. Actually, the male sex was getting pretty seriously trashed in the conversation in my dad's Buick. Didi was miffed that Todd had to attend his great-aunt's birthday party tonight (what a prince). And Jennifer was complaining about a recent bad breakup with a boyfriend.

"Men bite," she decided. "No offense, Ricky. I refuse to waste my youth on some guy whose idea of a good time is an all-day *Baywatch* marathon. I've got a new rule. From now on, it's all about me."

"That wouldn't work for me," said Didi. "Todd's pretty used to being the center of attention."

"That's a quarterback thing," I put in. "You guys need to date more kickers. Whoa!" I jammed on the brakes. We were still three blocks from Jake's house and already the streets were lined with cars. The parallel-parking jobs were a drivers'-ed. teacher's nightmare. Nelson Jaworski's pickup was half on the sidewalk, two inches from a fire hydrant. But it still managed to jut out far enough in the road to make it a tight squeeze to get between him and the idiot across the way who was four feet from the curb.

Didi was impressed. "There are a million people here! Who is this Jake?"

"Probably a jerk," decided Jennifer. "Anybody this happening has got to be full of himself."

"You're wrong," I said, parking behind a rusty Honda that was blocking someone's driveway. "Wait till you meet him."

As we headed for the front door, the van from Dante's Pizza pulled up. Out came an army of delivery boys, each with a stack of flat boxes. I recognized Kevin Fontaine from school.

He saw me too. "Hey, Rick, whose house is this? It's the fourth Friday in a row where everything we bake comes straight here! What's going on?"

"It's Jake, the new long-snapper for the Broncos," I replied. "He's got a way with parties."

"I thought the army was camping here or something," Kevin called back. "Seventeen pies, cash on the nose, and always a great tip."

"Does the army travel with a keg?" I asked smugly.

His eyes widened. "Sounds like the money spot."

"Want me to introduce you?" I asked.

"No time," he replied, climbing back in the van. "We've got nine orders on hold because of this." And Dante's Pizza roared off.

When I opened the front door, the blast of music almost blew us back out to the road. The house was even more crowded than it had been the week before with Fitzgerald High's beautiful people at frantic play. But the feeling was the same—in all the world, there was only one place to be, and this was it.

I could tell the girls were impressed because Jennifer couldn't think of a single obnoxious thing to say. I pointed them in the direction of the keg, yelled something about going to the bathroom, and ran off to warn Todd.

I almost went crazy finding him, not because he was hiding, but because the place was so jammed. It didn't help that some junior had brought his pet boa constrictor, Victor, which was scaring the daylights out of people. And I count myself among them. Picture this: you round the corner into the hall and come face-to-fang with a cold-eyed reptile whose head is bigger than yours. It was a good thing the stereo was so loud, because I'm pretty sure I screamed. I doubt I was the only one.

I finally ran into Todd shmoozing around the back porch. He was with Melissa again, which was a real risk. Not only was Nelson not passed out yet, but he actually seemed to be seeing single.

"Hi, Rick," slurred Melissa, who was barely seeing at all, as far as I could tell.

"Hey, Melissa. Todd, I need to talk to you."

"Rick," he mumbled through Melissa's big hair. "Chill out, man."

"This is important!"

But Todd was in that stubbornly cheerful party mood that refuses to deal with anybody who isn't in a similar state of mind.

"Sorry, Rick. I can't talk to you until you've had at least one beer. Those are the rules."

There was no time for pussyfooting around, so I just blurted it out. "Didi's here."

He jumped away from Melissa like she was carrying the plague. "Didi? Here? How?"

"Jake asked me to bring Jennifer," I admitted. "But then Didi tagged along because you told her you were busy."

"I can't believe you did that!" As I'd predicted, this was all my fault. "What am I going to do? I'm screwed!"

"Hey!" Melissa was miffed. "What am I— chopped liver?"

She tried to drape herself over him again. He shoved her away so hard that she flipped over the porch railing and landed flat on her back on the grass.

Before I could react, a couple of guys from the track team played follow the leader, as if Melissa had taken her leap on purpose. Cheering and snickering, they hurled themselves off the deck, landing perilously close to poor Melissa.

I ran down to where she lay, winded and sobbing. I was pretty amazed to see Todd still standing there, unmoved and unmoving.

"Get over here!" I hissed at him.

But the only thing on his mind was this mess with Didi. He barely even noticed that Melissa was there. As he walked back inside the house, I recognized his game face. It was fourth and goal, and Todd Buckley was going to fight for Todd Buckley.

I got Melissa calmed down and cleaned up, and released her into the wilderness. I wasn't afraid that she'd say anything to Nelson. How could she, after all, without making herself look bad?

I made better time getting back to the living room. The snake guy was on his way upstairs. I could see Victor the constrictor threading himself in and out of the struts of the banister.

Coming down the stairs was our gracious host, his Polo wardrobe slightly denim-ized with some Abercrombie accents. He was his affable self, shaking hands, slapping backs, and exchanging a few words here and there. I couldn't help noticing that while he talked to everybody, he didn't really talk to anybody—not more than "How's it going, baby? Good to see you!" He didn't even flinch when he saw the boa. He just held out his beer and let the forked tongue take a couple of tastes. Now, how cool was that?

I met him at the bottom of the stairs. "Another great party, Jake."

"Hey, baby." He was talking to me, but he seemed to be looking over my shoulder.

"Jennifer's by the pizza table," I supplied. "She brought her friend Didi."

Maybe it was the light, but for a second it looked as if tanned, confident Jake Garrett went white to the ears.

"That's okay, isn't it?" I added. "You said you wanted fresh blood, remember?"

"It's great!" he said a little too quickly. "Are they having a good time? Do they know anybody here?"

"Didi's Todd's girlfriend," I said. "She knows a lot of people. Come on, I'll take you over."

By the time we got to Jennifer and Didi, Todd was already with them. He might have been a good quarterback, but he was a lousy liar.

". . . so they rushed Aunt Sophie to Mercy Hospital. She's okay, but they had to cancel the dinner."

Didi looked suspicious. "Why didn't you go to the hospital?"

"Oh, I did," Todd explained. "But her room was too small. You know—with the whole family there. So I called you, and your mom said you were at a party. I took a gamble and came here looking for you."

It wasn't such a bad story. But the way Todd told it, it was obviously one hundred percent bull.

Jennifer looked totally disgusted. "You know what I think—"

Her friend cut her off. "I don't want to know." You could almost see the wheels spinning inside Didi's exquisite head. She was trying to bend and twist Todd's story until it fell into a shape she could believe.

I'd never had a steady girlfriend. But if swallowing this kind of crap was part of a relationship, then it was pretty pathetic.

I figured it was time to change the subject. "Jennifer, Didi, I want you to meet Jake Garrett."

Jennifer looked Jake up and down like a horse trainer checking out a new thoroughbred. And, man, he must have passed with flying colors, because she actually smiled. "Hi. Fantastic party."

He never even looked at her. Our host only had eyes for Didi.

"Hi, Jake." She was working hard to force Todd's story out of her mind. "It's funny. I used to know a guy named Jacob Garrett."

He gave her the Jake smile with both barrels. "It's been a long time, Didi."

chapter
four

"It's you!" Her perfect eyes widened in surprise. "Jacob, you look so—different!" She turned to Todd excitedly. "Jacob used to go to McKinley! He was my math tutor! If it wasn't for him, I'd still be in tenth grade!"

Todd seized on it like a drowning man who had just found a life preserver. "Jake's our new long-snapper," he beamed, putting an arm around Jake's shoulder. "He's going to be a great asset to the Broncos."

Didi was blown away. "You look *awesome!*" she told Jake. "And this is *your* party?"

He nodded. "I enjoy having a few friends over."

"I like big parties," Jennifer commented. "You

don't have to remember anybody's name."

Didi was taking a walk down memory lane. "Remember the time I had that test, and we studied by the pool, and you put sunscreen everywhere, but you forgot your nose?"

Jake nodded. "Quadratic equations."

She looked blank. "Huh?"

"That's what the test was on—quadratic equations."

"Oh, right," she said. "I remember my folks were out of town, but they left me their credit card. We ordered so much Chinese food that the bill was, like, two hundred dollars. And you got the idea to take the leftovers to a homeless shelter."

"And the homeless rejected the moo goo gai pan," laughed Jake. "They loved the ribs, though. And the sweet-and-sour chicken balls."

A bloodcurdling shriek cut through the loud music of the party.

Jennifer jumped. "What was that?"

"I think somebody just saw Victor," I remarked.

The girls wanted to take a look at the snake, so Jake walked off with one on each arm.

As soon as they were gone, Todd practically melted with relief. "Oh, man, that was close!

She bought it, right? I'm out of the woods?"

"Either way, you'd better keep your nose clean," I told him. "And you might want to apologize to Melissa for putting her in the dirt."

He looked ashamed. "Listen, Rick, I'm sorry I got on your case about this. I just really freaked out when I heard Didi was here." He grimaced. "The lousy part is that Didi's going to want to come *every* week now that it turns out she knows Jake. There must be some way around it!" The expression of concentration on his face would have been funny if it hadn't been so awful.

"I know," I suggested sarcastically. "Why don't you put out a contract on her? Then you won't have to worry about *any* week."

He looked pained. "Thanks a lot. I'm opening up to you as a friend, and all you can do is make bad jokes."

"*Broncos!*" came a bellow. A group of football players headed by Nelson swooped down on us, snatched up their fearless leader, and carried him off on their shoulders. Anyone in the way was either brushed aside or trampled.

I watched as the king accepted the adulation of his royal court. He was off the hook with Didi and riding high again. Yet I was the one feeling relieved. If Todd had gotten himself dumped

over this, the guy would have had a new girlfriend in about three minutes. But the stink of
having let him down would have followed me
around forever. He held all the cards, and I held
diddly-squat. It had always been that way. It
probably always would be.

Left on my own, I did a little walkabout. On
closer inspection, the party wasn't exactly the
same mix of people as the week before. Fresh
blood, Jake called it. Interspersed with the regulars were a handful of slightly edgier people—
body piercing, dog collars, green hair, black
leather. I saw the kid they called Poozer, who was
famous for cleaning his fingernails with a razor-
sharp army-surplus bayonet. He was currently
on suspension for throwing a punch at Mr.
DiPasquale, one of the assistant principals. There
was a nineteen-year-old who had taken a couple
of years off to travel around as a roadie for a ska
band. He was back to finish up a few classes for
his diploma. There was Phil Braggett talking to a
couple of girls. He was laying it on thick about
how he just got back from a few months in juvie
for some exotic, but nonspecific crime. He had a
great tan, though, which most people behind
bars don't get. I personally suspected he'd been
at his rich family's place in Palm Beach.

If Jake had hand-selected the newcomers, he couldn't have done a better job. Just by adding ten or fifteen people, he'd changed the whole feel of the party the way a great chef can make food come alive with a tiny dash of spice. Yet the selection was a careful one. Jake had invited kids who brought with them an air of toughness without actually inviting any really tough kids. There were guys who hung around drugs, but no dealers. There were guys who could fight, but probably wouldn't. There were guys who looked like they belonged in the East Village, or Venice Beach, but when push came to shove, they were suburban teenagers at a party.

Hands reached around my head and clamped over my eyes. I already knew it was Jennifer. She did this to me at least once every time we were together. I had to "guess."

"Is it the illegitimate love child of Buffy the Vampire Slayer and Mussolini?"

"Right!" she removed her hands and came to stand in front of me. "I swear to God, Ricky, this is the best party I've ever been to. They've got a game of strip Twister going on in the basement!"

I brightened. "Anybody losing?"

"Just Dipsy, but I don't think he's in the game. He's kind of passed out on the pool table with his head in a bag of Cheez Doodles. And he's got no pants on."

I remembered last week. "The football team probably stole them." I looked around. "Where's Didi?"

She shrugged. "Jake's giving her a tour of the house. I sure wasn't going to waste a good buzz looking at somebody's wallpaper."

"Because it's all about you," I finished.

She beamed. "Ricky, that's why I hate men. None of them can ever compare with you. Let's dance."

We squeezed into the pack of gyrating bodies and swayed in the same direction as everybody else. You couldn't move any other way—not unless you wanted to get coldcocked by a flying elbow. We must have looked like a wheat field on a windy day.

We were right in front of the speakers so Jennifer had to shout to be heard. "How do you think Jake pays for all this?"

I just shrugged.

"He's *your* friend," she persisted. "Food, beer—getting this place cleaned up must cost a few bucks. Not to mention his clothes. Does he have a job?"

I shook my head. "No time. He's got football

practice every day. Maybe he's got a trust fund or something."

"Ricky," she chided. "Look around. It's a pretty big house, but it's not an estate. What's Jake got going?"

"Will you give it a rest?" I complained. But deep down, I knew she had a point. I had a sneaking suspicion that the answer had something to do with those little white envelopes our host had collected at Throckmorton Hall.

The action seemed to be escalating. At around eleven, Corinne Gardner's Sweet Sixteen party showed up, twenty strong, dressed to kill, and determined to make up for a three-hour deficit in drinking. They brought with them a partially melted six-foot ice swan. In no time at all, there was an army of people all over it, trying to re-shape it with their tongues. I noticed Todd and Melissa in there, laughing hysterically, and obviously friends again.

It was around that time that Nelson fell down the stairs. He took three people with him, and it was a miracle that we didn't have to send for a fleet of ambulances. Though Nelson did knock out a tooth, which was found thirty feet away in the dining room.

At midnight, Kevin Fontaine burst through

the door with the entire staff of Dante's Pizza, just closed up.

"We delivered to nine parties tonight," Kevin informed me, "and this is the only one worth going to." He gawked at the writhing mass of swan-lickers. "This is the place to be."

It was pure insanity. By one A.M., the place was so crowded I thought the walls would split open. A bunch of football players were doing jumping jacks in the backyard in the pouring rain just to prove they were tougher than Liberty, our week-one opponents.

Some wise guy must have taken control of the music, because the CD player was off. Now the speakers blared out Jake's dad's old vinyl Beach Boys records at 45 r.p.m. In all the craziness, it sounded kind of good, like Munchkins on a caffeine buzz. There were twice as many dancers as before.

It took the laws of physics to put an end to the festivities. Shortly after three, the keg began hacking up foam. And by that time, the last piece of pizza had either been eaten or mashed into the carpet. The party was over.

It didn't break up right away, though. There was still a lot to go. There were some huge battles over car keys, to keep them in the hands of people who were fit to drive. Couples who had found their way into secluded areas were reappearing, looking bedraggled and sheepish.

The football calisthenics squad trooped back in, tracking most of the mud in the yard through the kitchen and living room. They were slapping hands, bonking heads, and screaming about their awesome workout. I knew perfectly well that on Monday, when Coach Hammer lined them up for calisthenics, they were going to grouse and moan like he was asking them to dig a tunnel to China with a shrimp fork.

I caught Jennifer in the kitchen, making out with the starting power forward of the basketball team. I felt a faint twinge of jealousy, but my Jennifer aspirations had been dead since sophomore year. Anyway, there didn't seem to be much to it. They didn't bother saying goodbye to each other.

She looked at me defiantly. "I don't even like him."

I shrugged. "I didn't say anything."

"I felt like kissing someone, okay? If I want to do something, I do it. That's the way it works now. It's all about me."

"Great," I yawned. "Everybody's leaving. Is Didi coming with us or with Todd?"

No sooner were the words out of my mouth than Jake and Didi stepped out of the laundry room, each with an armload of bottles for recycling.

I blinked and checked my watch. "Have those two been hanging out *all this time*? That's, like, six hours!"

Jennifer looked at me pityingly. "If you were Didi, would you spend the night listening to Todd put the finishing touches on the lamest lie since 'Nicotine is not addictive'?"

"Yeah, but the guy was her math tutor two years ago! They have nothing in common except Chinese food and quadratic equations!"

"Didi," called Jennifer. "We're leaving. Need a ride?"

Didi looked around. "Has anybody seen Todd?"

I'd seen Todd—chasing Melissa around the upstairs hall. The big question was, had Nelson seen him?

Todd appeared around the corner of the dining room. "Right here, Dee. Ready to go?"

Didi took a step toward him and was almost mowed down by a blur shooting up the basement stairs.

"Where are my pants?" howled Dipsy.

I looked to the ceiling fan, but it was clear.

Dipsy ran all over the house, his chunky derriere wagging in bright orange boxers. You'd think that after last week, the guy would know enough to put on less flashy underwear. I mean, nobody could resist reaching out a hand or foot and taking a swipe at that king-size Day-Glo butt.

Finally, Dipsy tracked down his tormentors from the Broncos and begged and pleaded for his pants. When that didn't work, he started shouting. And the words coming out of his mouth had nothing to do with coral reefs just then. He hurled every curse in the book at the bigger, stronger football players.

The situation had its humorous elements, but really, it was a pretty tense moment. I mean, pudgy Dipsy wouldn't have lasted five seconds in the ring with those guys. By the time they got through with him, there'd have been nothing left but a Teletubby cowlick and a tiny grease spot between the pizza stains on the carpet.

Then, all at once, the players were laughing their heads off, slapping him on the back and congratulating him like he'd just scored a game-winning touchdown. In great good humor, they told him his cargo pants were hanging from the exhaust pipe of the water heater in the basement.

When he went down to get them, he had about thirty spectators hot on his heels.

We all saw the pipe at the same time. No pants.

"They evaporated!" cried one of our wide receivers, which wasn't a bad joke for this late into the morning.

Well, the football players—they were practically hysterical. They were rolling on the cement floor of the furnace room.

"Swear to God!" howled Kendrick Jones, a linebacker. "That's where we put them!"

"Come on, guys," wheedled Dipsy. "I can't go home without my pants."

"Well, they couldn't have gotten up and walked," reasoned Jennifer.

Then we saw them. And for a moment it looked as if they really had gotten up and walked. Or at least crawled. They were slithering across the floor, legs spread wide.

The first screams probably came because Dipsy's pants seemed to have taken on a ghostly life. But when we realized what had actually happened, the yelling got even louder. Victor the constrictor had somehow crawled up one leg and down the other, and was making a break for it disguised as cargo pants.

And then Todd Buckley showed the main

advantage of being the first citizen of a high school. In the middle of all that chaos, he turned to Victor's owner and said, "This is getting boring. Pick up your snake and go home."

And that's exactly the way it unfolded. Guys got their girlfriends calmed down; girls assured their boyfriends that they had been macho enough in the crisis; and we all filed upstairs for the exit.

Didi left with Todd, and Jennifer and I headed out a few minutes later.

I paused at the door. "You've got a monster cleanup job here," I told Jake. "I can drop Jen and come back to give you a hand."

Relaxed as always, Jake just laughed it off. "Everything's taken care of, baby. I've got it covered."

Outside, the rain had settled into a cool mist.

Jennifer breathed a world-weary sigh. "Another boring Friday night. Nothing ever happens around here."

We looked at each other and cracked up laughing.

As we ran for the car, I noticed that Mrs. Appleford's upstairs bedroom light was on next door. There she sat at the window, scowling at the departing guests.

chapter
five

I ALWAYS WENT jogging during football season. But on Saturday, my "morning" run didn't start until noon. I wasn't very energetic, either. I consoled myself with the knowledge that a whole lot of people felt worse. I wouldn't have wanted to have Nelson Jaworski's head right now, and not just because it was full of rocks.

I made a point of running past the Garrett house, and what I saw in that picture window stopped me dead in my tracks. There, with a broom in one hand and a vacuum cleaner in the other, slaved the host with the most, Jake Garrett.

I was blown away. When Jake said the cleanup was all taken care of, I pictured a cleaning lady.

Or maybe a professional service where a truck-load of guys shows up at your house, and an hour later, you wouldn't be able to tell there'd ever been a party. In a million years I never would have dreamed that he was planning to do it all by himself. I mean, that house was a bomb crater!

I rang the bell, but I didn't wait for him to answer. The door wasn't locked, so I barged right in.

"Jake, what's going on?"

"Oh, hey, baby." He was trying to be his old cool self, but it wasn't quite coming off today. He looked harassed, exhausted, and above all, stressed.

"Last night you said you didn't need any help."

He scrubbed at a sticky stain on the floor. "Last night I didn't. But this morning my father called from Kansas City. He's on an earlier flight. He'll be here in an hour."

"Oh, boy." I grabbed a garbage bag and started stuffing in plastic cups and pizza-stained paper plates. It was one of those cleaning jobs where the more you work, the messier it seems to get. You pick up a napkin, but that only reveals the mashed-up cupcake underneath it. And that's pretty discouraging when the clock is ticking, and Jake's dad is getting closer by the minute. I filled four giant trash bags in the living room alone.

Then I got a peek into the kitchen. San Francisco must have looked like this after the big quake.

"We need more garbage bags!" I called into the dining room, where Jake was hanging curtains that had been ripped down during the night's festivities.

"Try the pantry," came the mumbled reply from a mouthful of drapery hooks.

I was lucky I even found the pantry behind all those pizza boxes.

By the time I ran up the stairs to check the second floor, there were eleven garbage bags standing out by the curb. Jake was rolling the empty keg out to hide in the garage, and Mr. Garrett was only fifteen minutes away.

Except for the plastic cups, which were strewn like leaves in October, the upstairs was in decent shape. I had to make all the beds, but I only filled one more bag up there.

I paused in the hall. Jake's room was unlocked, the door hanging slightly ajar. Well, I had to sneak a look. A guy's room is a mirror into his soul, and these days, Jake's was the hottest soul in town. Besides, a smart kid like Jake ought to know that putting a deadbolt on something only makes people twice as determined to get inside.

I don't know what I expected to find in there. Definitely nothing X Files, like shrunken heads or a stockpile of machine guns. But I was disappointed to see an ordinary room, maybe a little on the cluttered side. I mean, this was Jake Garrett, the guy who appeared out of nowhere and plastered his name onto the lips of every kid at Fitz. His parties were the talk of the school. Girls he'd never met stuck Post-it notes with their phone numbers on his locker, hoping to be invited to his next Friday-night bash. Freshmen made themselves look important by being able to identify the Garrett BMW in the parking lot. College guys treated him as an equal. He was an absolute star, in his own way, every bit as big as Todd Buckley. After all, most schools had a big-man-on-campus quarterback. But Jake was something that nobody had seen before or ever expected—cool, mysterious, *different*.

I poked around, but there wasn't much to see. On his desk sat a delivery menu from Dante's Pizza—tool of the party-throwing trade. There was also a neatly printed college essay by someone named Nancy Outerbridge. At the top was written *Term Paper, Physics 103, The Abiotic Synthesis of Organic Compounds.* Now, where had *that* come from?

I opened the drawer and peered inside. A trophy topped with a gold chess king gleamed up at me. JACOB GARRETT—MCKINLEY GRAND MASTER, 2001 was engraved on the base.

Hidden talents.

Suddenly, I heard cursing from downstairs.

I pulled up short, feeling like a kid caught with his finger in the cookie jar. I scrambled out into the hall, leaving the room more or less the way I'd found it.

"What's wrong?" I called over the banister.

"We forgot the basement!"

I checked my watch. Five minutes!

We made a mad stampede for the basement. Frantically, we raced around, throwing cups and plates into garbage bags.

There was the sound of a car door. We froze. Through the casement windows, we could see a taxi pulled up to the curb. Someone was getting out.

Jake panicked. "My dad! Quick—help me fold up the Twister game!"

The big plastic sheet was draped over the couch. We each grabbed an end and pulled. If I didn't have a heart attack right then, I'll probably live forever. For there, asleep on the sofa, his pants clutched to his heart, lay Dipsy.

"Do you think he's been here since last night?" I blurted. It was one of those natural exclamations that sound pretty stupid when you have a minute to think about them. Like, Dipsy had gone home, gotten up bright and early, broken into Jake's basement, taken off his pants, and crawled under the Twister mat for a snooze.

Jake shook Dipsy savagely. "Get your pants on, baby! My dad's here!"

"Huh?"

Our luck, Dipsy wasn't a morning person. We had to shove him into those pants one leg at a time.

Upstairs, the door slammed. "Jake?"

"I'm in the basement, Dad!"

There were footsteps on the stairs. "Jeez, Jake, there are twenty green bags on our lawn. When's the last time you put out the garbage?"

And suddenly, there he was, the old Jake. An excuse was required, and the world's smoothest liar was rising to the occasion.

"Sorry, Dad. I'm doing a little house cleaning. A couple of guys are here helping me."

As it turned out, all Mr. Garrett wanted to do

was take a shower and collapse into bed. This was a good thing, because it took a pretty tired guy to miss the fact that Dipsy looked like he'd been rolled in pretzel crumbs.

"Good to meet you boys," said Mr. Garrett. "I'm glad to see that Jake's making friends."

I could feel my lips twitch. Making friends? He should have been there twelve hours ago!

And then Dipsy, king of the non sequiturs, wriggled uncomfortably and announced, "I think there's snake crap in my pants."

I saw Mr. Garrett's tired eyes pop open for a second, while he tried to figure out what Dipsy could possibly have meant by that. Finally, he yawned and said, "I've got to throw in a load of laundry before I sack out."

"Oh, I'll take care of that," Jake offered. "You get some rest."

"You're a great kid, Jake. Thanks."

It occurred to me that the reason why Jake was such a "great kid" was that the washing machine was still full of ice and wine bottles.

In the end, Dipsy's cargo pants went in with that load of laundry. So after spending the night in Jake's basement with no pants on, Dipsy spent the afternoon in the same condition. I have to say he looked totally at home wrapped in a blanket on the couch, staring at a documentary on the sleeping sharks of Isla Mujeres.

"You know," I told him, "if you don't like the way the players treat you, you shouldn't hang around them so much."

He looked mystified. "Who said I don't like how they treat me?"

"How could you like it?" I exploded. "They goof on you every minute, humiliate you in front of hundreds of people!"

His gaze never left the TV screen. "The remora bides its time on the coral reef—"

"Forget it," I interrupted. "I should have known better than to expect you to be serious."

"I *am* being serious." He was looking right at me now. "I'm a remora."

"You're an idiot if you keep letting those guys treat you like a clown!" I snapped.

His gaze was penetrating, and I felt ridiculous almost immediately. I was pretty sure he was thinking back to sophomore year. Nobody had stolen my pants that day. But as disses go, it was one of the big ones. If Dipsy hadn't been there for me, who knows how much of a fool I might have made of myself? Was I really in a position to lecture him?

"Sorry," I mumbled. "I just mean you deserve better, that's all."

He shrugged. "I had a good time last night. I'm having a good time today." He turned back to his sleeping sharks.

True enough. And if he didn't let the Broncos crack on him, he wouldn't have made the guest list in the first place. Maybe I wouldn't have either, if I didn't know how to kick a football.

It had been almost three hours since I'd interrupted my morning run to help Jake clean up. Suddenly I just needed to get moving again, to lose myself in the mindless simplicity of putting one foot in front of the other.

Jake saw me to the door. "You were a lifesaver today, baby. Tell you what. I'll take you to lunch this week."

I had to laugh. "It's a deal. What are we going to get—the chicken nuggets or the Salisbury steak?"

"Not the cafeteria," he scoffed. "What do you say to Lakeshore Steakhouse?"

"That's *downtown*!" I exclaimed. "Our lunch lasts forty-two minutes."

"Only if you go to next period," he pointed out. "Come on, it'll be fun. I know the owner."

This was too much. "Movie stars eat at that

place, Jake! No way do you know the owner of the hottest restaurant in the city."

"His daughter goes to Atlantica," he explained with a grin. "I've done her a couple of favors. I'll set it up for Monday."

Then he launched into a whole speech about how much he had enjoyed meeting Jennifer at the party. Man, I was *there*. He had barely said two words to Jennifer. He had spent half the night with Didi, reminiscing about the good old days of being her *math* tutor!

"That was a pretty close call with your dad," I said. "I guess you'd better take a few weeks off parties."

He looked surprised. "Wrong, baby. Friday night, same time, same station." And as I walked away shaking my head, he called after me, "Bring Jennifer."

chapter
SIX

THE E-MAIL WAS waiting on my computer when I got home on Monday afternoon, stuffed to the gills from a three-hour lunch:

> Dear Stud,
> Meet me in the usual place for
> hot sex and the meaning of life.
> —Warrior Princess

Jennifer. Even her e-mails drove me crazy. Ninety percent of the time I wished I'd never even met the girl. She was a good friend, no question about that. I could tell her things that I wouldn't say to anybody else. Yet I couldn't share the one fact that ate me up from inside every minute I was with her—that being just friends was killing me. And I was starting to ask myself if this relationship was worth it.

Sophomore year. Sooner or later, it always came down to that. Ever since puberty I'd been wondering if Rick and Jennifer, friends since birth, could turn into something more. I didn't have the guts—not really. But I forced myself to ask her out.

It wasn't exactly a romantic date. Apple picking at Steubenville Orchards. But it was a big deal for me. I had just gotten my license. It was my first solo drive. I had my dad's car, Jennifer at my side, tunes on the radio, and a clear road ahead. It would be wrong to say I was happy—I was too nervous for that. But on some level I appreciated the beauty of the moment.

It was Fitz's annual Saturday at Steubenville, so I knew we'd run into a lot of kids from school. Todd's was the first familiar face—he was the JV quarterback then, so we were friends through football. I was honestly glad to see him. I'd confided to him my feelings for Jennifer.

Todd turned out to be an even better quarterback off the field than on. As we hung out near the basket stacks, greeting friends and football acquaintances, he ran my offense perfectly, keeping the conversation rolling, and making sure I had the ball when I needed it. Jennifer was relaxed and laughing, and I was so grateful to my buddy Todd that I would have gladly taken a bullet for him.

Then came the apple cider. In my excitement, I must have chugged a gallon. And when I came back from my first bathroom trip, everything was different. Yeah, people were talking, chuckling, joking. But Jennifer and Todd were in their own little private universe within our group.

"Hey, guys. Miss me?"

There were a few greetings and good-natured insults. But Jennifer and Todd didn't even notice me. Soon they had backed away from our circle, forming a satellite conversation. The same invisible cocoon that kept us out seemed to crowd them in, so that Todd's hand touched her arm every time he made a point, and Jennifer's fingers brushed his chest as she responded.

I don't remember being that devastated at first. Instead, I looked at them with an almost clinical interest. So this was how people got together. No official pronouncement of romance. Just a guy and a girl gravitating toward each other and away from everybody else. It was simple but unstoppable, like the advance of a glacier. I would have been fascinated if my world hadn't been crumbling all around me.

When they took off together, it seemed totally natural. I actually gave them a wave and a "Have fun." What could I have said that wouldn't have made me look like an even bigger loser? As it was, everybody saw it happen.

I was so destroyed that I might have spent the whole day rooted to that spot. It was Dipsy who handed me the basket, and for the next four hours, we picked apples like it was a life-and-death struggle. We weren't together, precisely. We didn't talk much. But every time I turned around, there he was.

It wasn't until I was sulking at the restaurant, all alone at a table reserved for two, that it came to me: if it hadn't been for Dipsy, I probably would have fallen to pieces in front of my entire high school. I hadn't done anything before or since to deserve his loyalty. He just saw a guy who needed support, and he gave it. I'd never forget that.

The Rick and Jennifer saga was dead before it started, but Todd and Jennifer didn't last much longer. Todd subscribed to the Mount Everest school of womanizing. He went for Jennifer because she was there. Once she was back at St. Mary's, he was with another girl within forty-eight hours. As for Jennifer, who knows what was going on in her head? Maybe I didn't fully communicate to her that this was a real date. She never said a word to me about it, and I certainly wasn't going to bring it up. It was almost as if it hadn't happened.

I still wasn't sure if that was a good thing. If I'd told her what I thought of her back then, I might have had a little more self-respect. Then again, I probably wouldn't be walking into Starbucks under the pseudonym Stud to greet my Warrior Princess.

She was at her favorite table, nursing a Venti Mocha, extra foamy.

"Hail, Princess. How goes the war?"

"Shut up and get yourself a coffee. I want the dirt on Jake Garrett."

"Dirt?"

"You're the one he's wining and dining. Lakeshore Steakhouse—not too shabby."

News traveled fast in the suburbs. Todd to Didi to Jennifer. The cell phone is a wonderful invention.

I bought the smallest decaf they had and slipped into the chair opposite hers. "You already know the dirt. He was her math tutor two years ago, and maybe something more. They lost touch, and they met again Friday night at the party. Why don't you ask Didi?"

She frowned. "Didi won't say much. And you know how she loves to talk."

"Maybe she's covering up something kinky," I suggested. "Leather, chains, quadratic equations. Those polynomials can get pretty hot."

"Not a chance. Didi did say that Jake tried to get close a couple of times, but she hosed him right down." She added, "Hard as it is to imagine any girl saying no to Jake."

"What's he got that I don't have?" I retorted, only half joking.

She was patient. "Don't get all defensive. Even you have to admit Jake's the place to be right now."

"His parties are, sure."

"No, *he* is. The guy is like a walking zone of happening, and everybody wants to breathe the rare air. Nobody has that, not even someone as good-looking as Todd."

Thanks a lot, Jen. "So why did Didi say no?"

She shrugged. "She was already dating some senior—Jake was only a sophomore back then. Besides, he was her math tutor. I can't even picture Jake being *that*."

I thought back to the chess trophy in Jake's desk drawer. "He's smart."

"Yeah, well, whatever the reason, she said no." Jennifer dredged the bottom of her coffee with a stir stick. "I'll bet it makes Didi feel weird to see girls drooling over him."

I shrugged. "She's got Todd. He treats her like crap, but that seems to come with the deal. And anyway, Jake's over her."

She gave me a motherly look. "Sometimes, Ricky, you're like a hayseed in the big city. It's totally obvious he's still gaga about her."

I shook my head. "*You're* the one he always talks about," I argued. "It was you he wanted me to bring to his party. Didi only tagged along, remember?"

She rolled her eyes with an exasperation that plainly said it was a burden to have to explain things to a moron like me. "Everyone knows Didi and I are a package. He asked for *me* to get to *her*."

I sighed. "Jake may be the place to be, but he's no better off than two years ago. He's still nosing around someone else's girlfriend."

"When he could be nosing around me," she concluded wistfully.

I must have blanched, because she added, "I'm *kidding*. Come on, Ricky. You know you're the only man who'll ever rock my world."

Promises, promises.

chapter
seven

"**WHAT'S THIS I** hear about you and that new Garrett boy throwing wild parties?"

Mom accosted me the minute I set foot in the house on Tuesday—short practice day. I've heard a lot about our generation having such a cool crop of parents—former hippies, Woodstock, peace and love, that kind of thing. I happen to be descended from the only two children of the sixties who thought hippies were all flakes.

"Don't you think you'd notice if I had a party?" I countered. "For starters, there'd be a whole lot of bodies blocking the TV."

"Don't get smart with me, young man," she said sharply. "Mrs. Appleford complained that the Garrett boy has been keeping her up every Friday night."

"Mrs. Appleford complains every time the wind blows," I reminded her. "You said so yourself. Remember the time she caught us watering the lawn on an odd-numbered day?"

"But she told me you were mixed up in it," Mom protested.

"I'm the one she *recognized*," I explained, "because Dad thinks it's easier to be friends with her than to face the wrath of the sprinkler Gestapo. I was only at that party because Jake invited all the Broncos. It's totally his thing."

I could see I'd won her over. "I'm sorry, Rick. You know how awful Mrs. Appleford can be. She's got *me* feeling guilty because I sold Pete Garrett that side-hall Colonial."

Mom was in real estate, so she never used the word *house*. In her world, people lived in Colonials and Tudors and split-levels and ranches.

"You never told me you knew Jake and his dad," I put in.

"Well, I don't *know* them, really," she replied. "I don't think I exchanged three words with the father the whole time they were looking. He always seemed to be just back from one business trip and on his way to another. But the boy—he knew exactly what he wanted. I've never seen a high-school kid so determined. He absolutely insisted on being close to St. Mary's. I told him St. Mary's is an all-girls school, but he wouldn't listen. They passed up a fabulous ranch in Irvington to live near a school he couldn't go to—four bedrooms, absolutely charming, new windows, bucolic setting."

Over the years I've learned to decode Mom's real-estate speak. For example, *charming* meant small. *Bucolic setting* meant the yard was being choked by ancient trees that hadn't been pruned since World War II. That was still better than *classic*, which almost always indicated that the place was so old it was a miracle it hadn't collapsed yet. I wondered how Mom would describe the Garrett home now. Maybe the beer stains on the carpet counted as "old-world Bavarian atmosphere." If Dipsy happened to be lying around somewhere in his underwear, that would probably count as "delightful local color."

"Well, I trust you, Rick," my mother said finally. "And I trust your judgment."

"Thanks, Mom." And she trusted Mrs. Appleford, who had twenty-four-hour surveillance going on everybody in the neighborhood.

The doorbell rang. I looked out the peephole

and found myself staring into the flawless features of Didi Ray. Even through that fish-eye view, distorted out of shape, she was still awesome.

I threw open the door and instinctively looked for Jennifer behind her, or maybe Todd. But Didi was alone.

"Hi, Rick! How are you?"

Since when did she care how I was?

"Uh, fine. How are you?"

She grasped my hand, running her index finger back and forth across my knuckles. Now, I realize this isn't the most sexual gesture in the world, but Didi supercharged any atmosphere. The heat produced by a brief knuckle caress from her would have to be measured in *bases* with any other girl. I almost jumped out of my skin.

I had never seen Didi in my life without Jennifer or Todd around. We were friends—but only in a friend-of-a-friend kind of way. Now she was seeking me out, **alone**, for the first time ever, and I let myself think, just for a second, hey, why not? Maybe hell froze over, and it suddenly occurred to Didi that I was the man of her dreams. Maybe Todd needed to spend some quality time with his dear sick Aunt Sophie, now that the rest of the family had vacated her hospital room. It was a long shot, but so are lottery tickets, right?

"Come with me to the mall, okay, Rick?"

"Okay," I began tentatively. "Uh—how's Todd?"

"Great," she said brightly, but she had nothing to add to that subject. "I need you to help me pick out something special for Jennifer's birthday. She's the first of all of us to turn eighteen."

I frowned. "Yeah, in *December*."

"Who wants to get caught in all that Christmas craziness?" she persisted. "Come on. I've got my car."

As I climbed into the passenger seat of her Volkswagen Beetle, it still didn't make sense to me. Yeah, Jennifer and I were old friends, but Didi was practically her sister. Jennifer knew personal stuff about Todd that even I, a denizen of the same locker room, didn't know—and definitely didn't *want* to know. What help could I possibly be?

"How about a sweater?" I asked as we squealed out of the driveway. Didi had a heavy foot for a size six-and-a-half.

She looked completely blank. "For what?"

"Jen's present!"

"Hey!"

She stomped on the brakes. Only my seat belt kept me from going straight through the windshield.

"What is it?" I asked shakily.

"Isn't that Jake's house?" We had stopped at the Garrett's side-hall Colonial with the old-world Bavarian charm on the living-room carpet, and the dead rosebushes out back. "You know, from the party?"

"This is the place." I was kind of surprised she recognized it. Jake's home blended into the neighborhood without eighty cars triple-parked in front. I'd lived here all my life, and I sometimes got it mixed up with a bunch of other houses in our subdivision.

"Let's go say hi," she urged. "I want to thank him for such a great party."

"Okay," I said slowly. I wasn't sure Jake wanted to be thanked. Throwing parties was just sort of what he did. I couldn't imagine him not doing it.

Didi was already out of the Beetle and halfway up the front walk. But when I rang the bell she hung back, like she was accompanying me on a tedious errand.

Jake appeared at the door. "Hey—"

When he saw Didi skulking behind me, his

J. Crew smoothness evaporated, and his jaw dropped open and hung there. I turned to Didi, but all she could manage was a weak "Hi, Jake."

Maybe Jennifer was right, and these two never got down and dirty sophomore year. But there was definitely something between them. Something big.

This was turning into a stupid afternoon that was destined to get stupider. We're hemming and hawing on Jake's doorstep. Jake, who has recovered, is *hey, baby*-ing at light speed. Somebody needed to make a move, and it seemed like it had to be me.

"We were just on our way to the mall. Want to come?"

You'd have thought we were inviting him to jam with the Rolling Stones.

We left Didi's car at Jake's and took the Beamer. The whole way there, Didi stared at Jake as if she'd never seen anybody drive before. Jake was as frazzled as a sixteen-year-old taking his road test. From my spot in the back, I could see his eyes in the rearview mirror, nervously darting over to the passenger seat.

I supplied all the conversation. "We're looking for a birthday present for Jennifer. I'm thinking sweater. Jen's into clothes. Any ideas, Jake?"

He barely heard me. "What was that, baby?"

"I really love this car," ventured Didi, and Jake glowed all the way to underground parking.

It was the weirdest shopping trip I've ever been on. First of all, there wasn't any shopping. To be honest, I'm not sure Jake and Didi even noticed they were in a mall. The place was packed with the after-school crowd, but the two of them were in their own private universe.

I pointed. "Want to hit Banana?"

They looked blank.

I was getting exasperated. "For Jen's present!"

"I trust your taste," Didi assured me. She plucked her Visa card out of her pocketbook and tossed it in my direction.

I snatched it out of the air. "Where are you guys going?"

"Take it easy, baby," soothed Jake. "We'll meet you back here."

"When?" I cried.

But they had already melted into the crowd.

What could I do? I picked out a Banana Republic sweater and stuck it on Didi's Visa— her dad's account, so I didn't sweat the price too much. It took about seven minutes. They weren't back yet, so I settled on a bench.

An hour later, I was still sitting there.

I was fuming. What the *hell* was going on?

A middle school kid on a skateboard, slaloming through the crowded mall, gave me a sympathetic shrug as he rolled by.

This was unbelievable. Didi was Todd's girl-friend. Yeah, I might let my imagination get ahead of me for about a millionth of a second when she's stroking my hand. But I always knew that, in the real world, dissing Todd Buckley was something that just didn't happen. Not even at the hands of Didi Ray.

By the time they got back, I was livid. "Do you have any idea how long I've been sitting here?"

Jake looked at his watch in amazement. "Sorry, baby!" I knew he was a world-class liar, but I don't think even he could fake such genuine surprise. "I thought it was more like—I don't know—twenty minutes!"

"We were talking about our McKinley days," added Didi with a conspiratorial smile at Jake.

"What part?" I muttered. "The Pythagorean theorem or the Cartesian geometry?"

When Jake fumbled for his wallet to pay the parking guy, a couple of ripped movie tickets popped out. One of them fluttered to the floor of the backseat. I squinted in the dim light of the underground garage. It was from that afternoon—the four-thirty showing of *Seven Samurai.*

They went to a movie? My bewilderment was the only thing keeping my rage in check. Who goes to see a fifty-year-old art flick that's all in Japanese, and then leaves halfway through?

I assumed Jake would take Didi back to her car, but we drove right past the Garrett place to my house.

"Thanks for picking out the sweater, Rick," Didi gushed. "Jennifer's going to love it."

I was glad she liked it so much, considering she never even took it out of the bag. I might have bought Jennifer a bulletproof vest for all she knew.

I got out of the car. "The next time you need a fashion consultant, call Tommy Hilfiger."

They didn't rise to the bait. Or maybe they just didn't notice it. The two of them were glowing.

"Good to see you, baby," Jake added. "Catch you at school tomorrow." And the Beamer whispered off back to Jake's.

Jennifer was right. I *was* a hayseed in the big city. I should have cut out on that "shopping" expedition when we were still on Jake's front stoop.

You don't grow up in constant terror of Mrs. Appleford without learning a thing or two about the art of neighborhood espionage. A little after nine, I took a casual stroll around the block.

Didi's car was still parked in Jake's driveway.

chapter
eight

ALL WEEK I waited for it to hit the fan. Todd Buckley gets dumped. That was the equivalent of a coup d'état at F. Scott Fitzgerald High. I couldn't imagine a hotter story.

Every day I walked through the double doors expecting to hear an excited buzz, like the time Phil Braggett cracked up his old man's Alfa Romeo and put himself in intensive care. Or the fake-sympathetic delighted whispering when everybody found out that Jerrie Javitz was pregnant—and the even juicier reprise a few weeks later, when they realized that she wasn't anymore.

There was nothing. Just the delivery guy from 1-800-4BAGELS, camped out in front of my locker, bearing a Deluxe Breakfast on the Fly. A peace offering from Jake, I think.

I recognized the kid as he poured my O.J. "Throckmorton Hall, right?"

He seemed surprised. "How did you know?"

"And Jake did you a favor?"

"How happening is that guy?" the A.U. student marveled. "You should have seen the smoking chick at his other drop-off. Girlfriend or something."

Somebody's girlfriend.

Speaking of Todd, he continued to be his usual arrogant self. He had taken to identifying every single adult male visitor to the school as a college scout here to observe the Broncos practice. That included the bagel guy, the superintendent of schools, and the coveralled plumber who came to Roto-Rooter Fitz's main sewer connection.

"Don't take it so hard," I advised when the man departed, leaving Todd's free-agent status intact. "You don't want to play for a team that's already in the toilet."

Todd just smiled serenely. "So he's not the guy. But he'll be here—right in the front row."

If this was someone who had just been kissed off by Didi Ray, then he had to be the greatest actor in the history of high school. And

Todd despised the drama club, because he was convinced all the guys in it were gay.

I was dying to talk to Jake, but he was difficult to nail down. At practice, Coach Hammer had us working on field-goal kicking, and the holder was Todd, so that was out. And as soon as I got home from school, there was Didi's Volkswagen, parked alongside the Beamer in the Garrett driveway. Well, I sure wasn't going to walk in on that love nest.

I needed to run into the guy at school, but that was easier said than done. Jake wasn't in any of my classes. And when I started asking around, not a single person I knew had a course with him. So on Thursday I went to see Danny Nash, who worked in the guidance office. Danny did favors for a lot of athletes in return for varsity hats and shirts he could use to impress girls from other schools. Today, however, it wasn't any Fitzgerald souvenir that Danny had his eye on. He wanted what everybody wanted—an invitation to Jake's party the next night. I couldn't guarantee *that*, of course, but Danny saw the logic. How could I ask Jake if I couldn't even find him?

Danny pulled Jake's schedule, and I realized why nobody was in any of his classes. Jake

Garrett was enrolled in honors everything! If there was such a thing as enriched lunch, he would have been in it.

At three o'clock, I waited for him outside advanced-placement computer programming.

Jake looked a little sheepish when he saw me. "Hey, baby. I figured I'd catch you at the field."

The Broncos' first game was on Saturday, so Coach Hammer was fanning the flames of student interest with a good old-fashioned pep rally.

"We can head over there together," I said as we started in the direction of the exit. "Hey, I never pegged you for advanced placement."

He gave me a healthy dose of the Jake smile. "Dad's idea, not mine. To save money in college."

I shrugged. "No crime in being smart."

"That's debatable," he muttered in a low voice. Then, louder, "It's a joke."

"Is that where you've been all week?" I probed. "Studying?"

He stopped and regarded me intently. He was trying to figure out if I knew. "Didi"—it took a lot of effort for him to say her name, but once it was out, the rest followed easily—"has been coming over. A lot."

I nodded. We pushed open the double doors and ran for the football field.

We were the last to get suited up. Yes, Coach Hammer made us attend this charade in full pads. I guess we were more inspiring pep-wise if the kids saw us with some extra bulk.

Actually, the old snot-and-mustard had a pretty good turnout that day. One of our grandstands faced due southwest, and it was a warm, late-September afternoon. To find a better sunning opportunity, you'd have to go to Barbados.

Surprisingly, our most vocal devotee was, of all people, Dipsy, who had declared himself kind of an unofficial cheerleader. Mascot might be a better word, because, at a Broncos event, he was as out of control as any wild animal. And for someone who hardly spoke at all except for quiet, nonsensical lectures on marine biology, the guy could shout down a stadium full of people.

"ALL THE WAY, TEAM! WE'RE GOING ALL THE WAY!"

It was pretty embarrassing for us players, especially at games, with visitors from other schools staring at him *and* us like we were from Pluto. But the Broncos, who raked Dipsy over the coals for everything else, never got mad at him for this. He was, after all, our number-one fan, and a crummy team needed all the supporters it could get. Personally, I could never quite figure out if Dipsy was being totally serious or just putting us on. He didn't strike me as the "rah-rah" type. My theory was that it was his revenge for a whole lot of teasing and practical jokes. But I kept my opinion to myself.

What the Broncos didn't have in talent they made up for in testosterone. The guys were putting on a great show, slapping butts, bumping chests, and bonking helmets. The smart ones kept their distance from Nelson, the self-appointed distributor of concussions. He put a shoulder into one of the running backs that knocked the kid flying, setting in motion a domino effect that took six or seven players to the turf.

Our fans went nuts.

"Hey! *Hey!*" barked the coach. "Save it for Liberty, you maniacs!" He was grinning. In football, the prevailing wisdom went that homicidal violence was a good thing, as long as it could be directed at the other team.

Jake and I, the latecomers, jogged into the fray. Since the coach was in a good mood, there was a lot of goofing around going on. Most of the guys' girlfriends were with them—except for the cheerleaders, who were bumping and grinding through their routines in a style better suited to rap videos that had been banned from MTV.

I blinked. There was Didi, hanging all over Todd, playing the perfect quarterback's trophy girl. She'd come from St. Mary's to support her man—as if she *hadn't* spent the better part of a week practically shacked up with Jake Garrett!

My mind went into high gear. Maybe I had the wrong idea about Didi and Jake. Maybe they were only getting together to plan a surprise party for Todd. (The millennium celebration didn't take that much preparation.) But one look at Jake's face told me all I needed to know: he thought Didi was his. Didi, apparently, thought otherwise.

For a moment I suspected that this pep rally was going to get memorable. I put a hand on Jake's shoulder. "Not here," I whispered. "And definitely not now."

His misery was so tangible that you could almost grab pieces of it out of the air around his head and shoulders.

"She's going to dump him, you know," he

said earnestly. "This is just so he looks good in front of the team."

I nodded noncommittally. Let me tell you, Todd looked *awesome* in front of the team. An ape would look good with Didi crawling over him.

"Listen, Jake," I said, trying to pick my words carefully. "Does it really have to be Didi? I know how hot she is, and that you two used to know each other. But there's something going on in that girl's head that neither of us understands."

"She doesn't even like him anymore," Jake went on, as if his words could erase what was happening. "She knows he cheats on her."

If Didi didn't like Todd anymore, she had a hell of a way of showing it. A smart kid like Jake should have been able to see that. Our long-snapper had a serious blind spot where Didi was concerned. In fairness, he wasn't the first guy with that problem, and he wouldn't be the last.

"You know, there are lots of girls who are dying to date you," I told him. "Your parties have made you the guy to know at school this year. The word is, Corinne Gardner's been talking you up. Remember her? The sweet sixteen? The ice swan?"

His eyes never left Didi in Todd's arms. "I didn't do all this for Corinne Gardner," he said absently.

"What are you talking about?"

He looked nervous. "It's just an expression, baby."

At that moment, the pep rally built to a noisy crescendo in which a few of the Broncos kicked the stuffing out of a huge plush wildcat, representing the mascot of the Liberty Lions. Nelson delivered the coup de grace with a golf club that took the head clean off and put it in the fifth row of bleachers. There it was reduced to molecules by Dipsy.

Coach Hammer must have been thrilled with all this, because he let the visitors hang out for a while before clearing the field for an abbreviated practice.

It seemed very casual the way Jake worked his way over to Didi. But I could see how smoothly he meandered from group to group, inviting people to "a little get-together" he was planning for the next night. He said it as if this had just occurred to him, and his Friday bashes weren't as regular as the tides.

"Jake!" cried Didi, delighted to run into an old friend. "Long time, no see!"

Remind me never to go to *her* eye doctor.

"Hey, Jake," Todd said warmly. "Party tomorrow night, right?"

I held my breath, waiting for Jake to take a swing at him, or at the very least, curse him out. Instead, Todd received a brilliant flash of the Jake smile.

"Same time, same station, baby."

chapter
nine

I MADE UP my mind to hit Jake's place early on Friday. It was going to be weird for him to host Didi and Todd, as well as a hundred and fifty of his nearest and dearest.

Around school, I had a reputation as Jake's best friend, believe it or not. I'd only met the guy two weeks before, but there was something about Jake that made things happen fast. Like his parties, he existed in an accelerated universe. A steak sandwich, a few bagels, and we were lifetime chums.

I have to admit I liked it. Jake was famous, so I was sort of famous too. We kickers don't get a lot of headlines.

And anyway, at Fitz, Todd was considered a friend of mine too. So the bar wasn't set very high.

I was surprised to find another car parked beside the Beamer in Jake's driveway. I rang the bell and let myself inside. There in the living room paced a college kid, Connor Somebody—or maybe Somebody Connor. He had been one of the envelopes in Marty Rapaport's room at Throckmorton Hall that day.

"Where's Jake?" I asked.

"Get in line, pal," he growled, tapping the foam out of the new keg, which was chilling in the wading pool. "He owes me first."

I headed for the stairs, and he glared at me. "Don't bug the guy. He's already three days late."

In the second floor hallway, I knocked politely on the locked door.

"I'm not finished yet," came a voice from inside.

"Jake, it's me. Rick."

"Rick!" The scrambling behind that closed door was frantic. He opened it just a crack, and this time the Jake smile didn't really come off. "You're early, baby. Why don't you have a beer downstairs? You remember Connor, right?"

I pushed it open and stepped inside. I wasn't copping an attitude, but I felt stupid standing there in the hall. "I've been in here before, Jake. On cleanup day."

"I'm a little behind schedule," he admitted sheepishly. "There are a few things I have to take care of before the party tonight."

"This better be brilliant!" came a bellow from downstairs. "If I wanted it lousy and overdue, I'd write it myself!"

My eyes traveled to the document under construction on Jake's computer screen. I couldn't make out the title, but the words *by Connor Danvers* were crystal clear.

Jake gave a nervous laugh. "I guess you've figured out my little side job."

I looked at him, bug-eyed. "How smart *are* you, Jake? You're writing people's *college* papers while you're still in high school?"

"I'm not that smart," he snapped back as if I'd just insulted him.

I remembered the procession of envelopes at Atlantica University. "How many of these things can you write?"

"Throwing parties is an expensive hobby," he admitted, "and I've got a taste for clothes. I was keeping on top of it okay. But lately I've been busy with—other stuff."

In other words, spending every waking moment with Didi had thrown him off his business schedule.

All I could manage was a shrug. "I'd help you, but I'm not much of an expert on"—I squinted at the screen—"quantum physics."

"Oh, that's okay, baby. Listen, do me a favor. Hang with Connor—make sure he doesn't freak out. Call in the pizza order for nine o'clock. And when people start to arrive, make sure they get drinks. Everything's fine so long as everybody's drinking."

Words to live by.

I put on the stereo loud. Not that there were any guests yet, but I didn't feel like taking the brunt of Connor's irritation with Jake. Actually, the Atlantica student had fallen into a holding pattern in front of the TV, watching a sumo wrestling match with the sound turned off.

I couldn't conjure a mental image of what it would be like when the first people showed up. By the time I'd arrived at the last two parties, the joint had been jumping. I couldn't imagine a handful of kids wandering around the empty living room, politely checking out the books on the shelves.

It didn't happen that way. Instead, nobody came for a long time. But around eight-thirty, I started hearing a lot of passing traffic on the street—which was weird. I'd lived here my whole life. Our block was an anonymous little crescent that went from nothing to nowhere.

I went to the window, and there they were— dozens of cars, circling at about ten miles an hour. Every now and then, one of them would slip into a parking space, and the rest would continue their languid orbit.

I was fascinated. It was like watching the mating dance of the great crested grebe, or something. Everybody wanted to come, but nobody wanted to be first. And the longer I watched them, the more improbable it seemed that anyone would ever get out of the car. In order for this traffic pattern to turn into a party, somebody was going to have to brave the forty-foot walk from the curb to Jake's front door with the collective eye of F. Scott Fitzgerald High on him/her.

In the end, it took an act of God. Too many teenage drivers, not enough road. Eventually, someone clipped someone else's taillight. A loud screaming match ensued between the rear-ender and the rear-endee. Soon there were forty peacemakers keeping them from going for each other's throats.

Then, all at once, the situation was defused, and the entire crowd headed as one for Jake

Garrett's living room. As acting host, I tried to greet them. I was lucky they didn't trample me.

The fact that Jake was nowhere to be found didn't bother anyone in the slightest. I doubt very many of them even noticed. I came to see that a party is a living, breathing organism that takes care of itself. I didn't have to worry about changing the CD. When it ended, the kid who cared the most became the de facto DJ. Someone was there to take in the pizza. Someone else lowered the lights when the dancing started.

Jake was right. Everybody was drinking, so everything was fine.

The usual suspects were trickling in as people continued to arrive. Nelson steered Melissa through the door about nine, and had thrown his first punch by 9:04—a misunderstanding with a sophomore who had inadvertently stepped on his foot. One of the hazards of these parties was that Nelson's size fourteen-and-a-half construction boots became harder to avoid as the house filled up.

I saw Dipsy with his head buried in a bag of caramel popcorn. As of nine-thirty, he still had his pants on.

Most of the Broncos were there by then, so

the obnoxiousness level was sky-high. Football players, at the top of the food chain, felt the need to act like the biggest jerks. They were followed by basketball players, wrestlers, hockey players, and so on down the line.

Speaking of the food chain, there was its apex, Todd Buckley, with the ever-faithful Didi at his side. A great shout went up from the Broncos in the room, and they surrounded Todd and bore him off in a flurry of affectionate noogies. There stood Didi, the hottest girl in anyone's imagination, alone and abandoned. At last, Todd had brought her to one of Jake's parties. He had stayed with her for about thirty seconds.

For her part, Didi seemed unperturbed. She wandered a little, greeting people and drawing admiring stares. Spying me, she rushed over, took my hand, and squeezed the two of us out among the crush of dancers.

This time I wasn't fooled. "Jake's busy," I informed her. "He should be down soon." I checked my watch. Jake had been working on this essay forever. If he didn't get a move on, Connor was going to kick in the lock and force-feed Jake his chess trophy.

But then I spotted Connor in a corner of the dining room, making out with one of the cheerleaders. So quantum physics was probably the last thing on his mind. Biology was now the subject of the minute.

"Does Jake know I'm here?" Didi asked.

The arrogance of that irked me a little. Yes, she was great looking. But did she think she gave off some kind of aura or vibe that would reach the guy from the opposite end of the house?

"If he was looking out the window," I said pointedly, "he probably saw you and Todd drive up."

If she got my meaning, she didn't show it. "When you see him, tell him I'm here." And she walked away. I had outlived my usefulness.

As I began to wander, I felt, rather than heard, a series of percussive pops coming from outside the open front door. There on the walk ducked and dove five freshmen boys. These uninvited unworthies were being pelted with lightbulbs from every lamp and fixture on the second floor.

"What are those geniuses up there going to do when they need to see something?" I commented to the spectator next to me.

It was Dipsy. "The ocean's deepest trenches form an inky world without sun, home to alien creatures that would rival any science-fiction movie."

I sighed. "Is that where the remoras live?"

He seemed genuinely thrilled that I'd remembered. "What goes on up there—lights would only get in the way."

"Look," I told him. "If you see any Broncos, just keep your distance. If they can't find you, they can't steal your pants."

He pretended to miss my point. "If my pants don't mind, why should you?"

"Jeez, Ricky!" Jennifer reeled in, interposing herself between Dipsy and me. She patted her hair, which gleamed with glass fragments. "Can you believe this?"

"Sorry," I grinned. "The artillery got a little carried away."

"Not that!" She dismissed the bulb shower with a wave of her hand. "A bunch of freshmen just tried to get in here! What do they think this is—gymboree?"

I led her into the kitchen and stood her by the garbage can while I brushed her off with a dishtowel.

She turned it into a sexual situation. "If you're trying to push my buttons, there are better ways to get the job done."

If only. But I had other things on my mind. "What's Didi's problem? Is she with Todd, or with Jake, or what?"

"She's with Todd, obviously," Jennifer told me. "This Jake thing is just, you know, a hobby. Like you're a lawyer for your job, but you play golf in your spare time."

"Who does she think she is—Tiger Woods?" I exclaimed. "She was here *all week*! Does Jake know she's golfing, not lawyering?"

"He's getting quality beyond his wildest dreams," she pointed out. "He's probably over the moon."

I didn't argue with her. Jennifer wasn't the warm and fuzzy type, but, as usual, her analysis of the situation was bang on.

Aloud, I just said, "I don't think that's the way Jake sees it. He's really head over heels."

She shrugged hugely. "Life's a big, cruel, scary thing, Ricky. We've all got our problems. Do you hear me complaining because all men are jerks?"

I let that one pass. No conversation went very long before turning into the World According to Jennifer. To use her words, it was all about her.

She did have one more thing to comment on.

Jake and Didi: "You think Didi doesn't know how Todd is when she's not around? Maybe some of this is payback."

"Get out of the way!" came a bellow.

The kitchen was invaded by a stampede of senior girls, carrying their boyfriends piggyback. I was astonished to see Melissa with the six-foot-five, two-hundred-sixty-pound Nelson up there. I thought of her and Todd sequestered in the bathroom. I wondered if Casanova realized that he could have more to fear from her than from Nelson.

With a thud that was audible even over the pounding music, Nelson's forehead made contact with the light fixture. The big lineman went down in a shower of plaster, bringing with him Melissa, the other piggybackers, and half the people in the kitchen, myself included. The light went out. The fixture hung by a single wire. By the time I managed to get up again, Jennifer had melted away into the throng.

I tried to escape into the hall and found it jammed. The party was approaching critical mass. You couldn't have crammed another body in there with a shoehorn. Some guy was playing tonsil hockey with the captain of the girls' tennis team. Not far away, a gaggle of his friends had formed a half circle, and were spitting at the back of his neck. From what I could see, they had found the range. Foam dripped down the back of his shirt. He must have been clammy and miserable, but he never stopped for a breath, never gave an inch for fear of letting the girl get away.

It was standard issue for a Garrett bash—the kind of semi-funny, semi-moronic stuff that had been going on for weeks in this house. Yet there was something different and vaguely unpleasant about it tonight. I took a good look at the slack-jawed, laughing faces. I didn't know these guys. They weren't from F. Scott Fitzgerald High. Word of the parties had begun to travel around town, and crashers were beginning to show up. They weren't ax-murderers or anything like that. They seemed to be pretty much the same pinheads that Fitz was turning out, and their entertainment choices were no shallower than ours. But there was a peculiar ugliness about strangers acting this way, rather than kids from our own extended family. I noticed a lot of other unfamiliar faces around the house. And while they weren't doing anything different from our homegrown rabble, they filled me with a sense of unease.

"Hey, baby—" Jake sidled up to me. His J. Crewness seemed to have been restored after his wrestling match with quantum physics. "Jennifer said Didi was here. Why didn't you tell me?"

"You seemed pretty stressed about that essay."

"That doesn't apply to Didi." He was talking to me, but his eyes were scanning the room and beyond.

"Listen, Jake," I said, "did you invite all these kids? There are people here I've never seen before in my life."

"Fresh blood," he explained absently, making his way to the stairs. The place was so crowded that he was never going to be able to spot Didi unless he gained some altitude.

I followed him up the first few steps. "Fresh blood is one thing," I argued. "But these guys could trash your house and not even have to look you in the eye on Monday morning."

Talk to the wall. He was one-hundred-percent gone from me. I followed his gaze and spotted Didi talking with some of the girls' volleyball team.

Then she noticed him too. Their eyes locked, and I swear the lights dimmed for a moment from the power surge. They began to move toward each other. They were separated by thirty feet, tops.

But a good four dozen revelers occupied the space between them.

I don't think Jake and Didi noticed. In their minds, they were the only two people in this jammed party house, and quite possibly the entire planet. Didi didn't look to me like she was playing weekend golf. This was lawyering of the highest order, an appearance before the Supreme Court.

As I watched them come together, I had a sense of two soldiers crossing an active battlefield to meet in the middle. Dancers gyrated, drinks spilled, play-fighters traded shoves, heavy bass shook the air. And through it all, Jake and Didi found each other on a Friday night in late September.

They didn't fall into a soulful B-movie embrace. In fact, they didn't touch each other at all. But you'd have to be drunk, dense, or totally self-absorbed not to notice the magnetism between them.

Todd was all three, but even he managed to figure it out. His face reddening, his scowl thunderous, he waded through the mass of humanity to confront the meeting at the bottom of the stairs.

He grabbed his girlfriend's arm. "Let's go, Didi. This party's boring."

A cherry bomb went off in the dining room, and a moment later, the student council vice president leaped high above the sea of heads, his dreadlocks on fire. It was out in a second, beaten down by a flailing pocketbook. But that didn't stop someone from emptying the kitchen fire extinguisher in the guy's face. Light, fluffy foam blanketed the remnants of seventeen pizzas.

"I'm not ready yet," Didi told Todd. "I want to stay."

He looked more surprised than annoyed. How often did Todd Buckley hear the word no? "Seriously," he said. "Let's get going."

"I'm having a good time," she insisted.

Jake put his two cents in. "I'll see that she gets home, baby."

"I bet you would," growled Todd. "Okay, we're staying." He stormed away.

On the surface, it was a fairly innocent exchange, one that maybe a handful of people noticed over the music and the craziness. But to this observer, the meaning was undeniable: Todd was vulnerable, and he knew it.

Jennifer appeared at my elbow. "You know what your problem is, Ricky? You don't know when to mind your own business. So Todd's a little bent out of shape. So what? I can't think of anyone who deserves it more than him."

She was probably right about the minding my own business part. Was my appointment book so empty that I had to stick my nose into other people's love lives to feel important? I was turning into the Mrs. Appleford of Fitz. Was it revenge against Todd that I was trying to savor—over what he'd done to me that day in the apple orchard? He'd stolen Jennifer, and justice required him to forfeit a girl too. If so, it was pretty sour revenge. I wasn't enjoying the spectacle of Todd getting burned. No, I was observing this the way you'd watch two out-of-control trains careening inevitably together—with a mixture of fascination and dread.

One thing was certain. I had never seen Todd "a little bent out of shape." This was uncharted ground. So I kept an eye on him. For the next half hour or so, he did a tour of the party, checking in with old admirers to remind himself that he was still the man. Our first game was tomorrow, so it was a good night to rev up enthusiasm for the old snot-and-mustard. Todd had them bonking heads and biting sofa cushions to work up their hatred of Liberty. Judging from the number of players around the keg, my teammates were also working up raging hangovers, which didn't bode well for game day. If Jake kept on having Friday-night parties, the really smart move would be to put money on our opponents all through the season.

Melissa was part of a group that had staked out the space under the kitchen table. There were four of them, a guy and three girls, smashing Ritz crackers with a ball peen hammer. They had no purpose for the mounds of beige dust they were creating. Yet they wore grimaces of intense concentration, as if they were splitting the atom.

When Todd found Melissa, I could almost see the lightbulb flashing over his head. It wasn't a dance of seduction. He just reached under the table, grabbed her by the arm, and dragged her through the hall and up the stairs. He didn't care who saw them. In fact, he was probably counting on word getting back to Didi. I don't know if he even thought about Nelson. I sure would have. The last time I'd seen Nelson, he was down in the basement, trying to tackle the five-hundred-gallon iron oil tank that stood next to the furnace. Todd was probably safe on that front.

I watched them from the bottom of the stairs.

Their previous three-minute maulings had taken place in bathrooms and closets. But Todd meant business this time. He hustled her straight into a spare bedroom and slammed the door.

I looked for Didi and Jake, but they were gone too.

It hadn't been much of a fun evening anyway, but that was the moment I stopped enjoying Jake's parties for good. All the madcap silliness just seemed kind of brainless and hurtful. Jake was crazy if he thought it made sense to let two hundred people, half of them total strangers, lay waste to his house. Didi wasn't worth it. Nothing was.

The front door burst open, and the party improbably absorbed seven more guests. Connor was there to high-five the newcomers, one of whom was the delivery man from 1-800-4BAGELS. This invasion was from Atlantica University.

"These girls go nuts for college guys!" Connor bawled. "Just show them your student ID and you're golden!"

There was a bloodcurdling scream from the basement, and a pack of Broncos burst up the stairs, faces shining with excitement and purpose. If they did to the Liberty defense what they did to the party guests as they bulled their way to the door, tomorrow was going to be a momentous day for Fitzgerald football. Kids were hitting the deck left, right, and center, including a couple of the A.U. guys.

I was bewildered until I saw the pair of jeans tucked under Kendrick's arm. And Dipsy was right on schedule, barelegged and humiliated in his fluorescent-blue skivvies.

I couldn't make out his exact words over the din. But since I'd heard them on two previous occasions, my mind easily filled in the blanks: "Come on, guys! Give me back my pants!"

About fifty people rushed outdoors to watch the half-naked, pudgy Dipsy try to catch up to four athletes in peak physical condition. The Broncos piled into an ancient convertible Chevy Malibu and started the unmuffled engine. Spearing Dipsy's jeans on the radio antenna, they pulled out into the street and began to inch along, the pant legs flapping like two flags on a diplomatic limousine. They rolled just slowly enough to keep poor Dipsy in the chase. He puffed along behind them, yelling, "Come on, guys!" at increasing levels of exhaustion.

Someone winged a half-eaten s'more at him, missing his phallic cowlick by inches.

The spectators were on the grass, rollicking with mirth. Some of them were laughing so hard that tears streamed down their cheeks. It was, I admit, one of the more hilarious sights I'd ever witnessed.

I didn't even crack a smile.

chapter
ten

COACH HAMMER'S PEP talk was designed to raise the dead. Which was a good thing, because the dead were pretty much who he had in the collection of hangovers in the locker room that Saturday afternoon.

Three-quarters of the team sat pale and stoic, like they were carved out of marble, while the coach ratcheted up his rhetoric in an effort to get a rise out of this statuary in shoulder pads. It wasn't enough that the Liberty Lions didn't respect us and thought we were pushovers. No, they were slashing our tires, urinating in our school halls, and burning effigies of our grandmothers. They were subhuman troglodytes who had to be snuffed out of existence for the good of all God-fearing people. And earth's last stand against this menace would be made on the gridiron this very afternoon.

"So I want you to get out there and fight!" Hammer rasped with what was left of his voice.

We came roaring to our feet, and Nelson Jaworski's simmering cauldron of testosterone reached critical mass. With a howl that could only be described as bestial, he picked up an eight-foot-long wooden bench and swung it at all our heads. We were alert enough to duck, and the blow struck a row of metal lockers. The bench shattered, and the lockers went down with a heavy clatter.

Todd, Kendrick, and I grabbed Nelson, and he shrugged us off as easily as he might have swatted a fly.

Still bellowing like a mad bull, he charged across the room and planted his helmet dead center on the chalkboard. The diagram of our pass defense disintegrated as the slate broke into hundreds of fragments.

The look of horror on Coach Hammer's face plainly said that this had never happened to him before. To rile a team to rage was something straight out of Coaching 101. But it had not occurred to him that the amount of emotion required to get an ordinary guy snarling and spitting would put a Nelson Jaworski over the edge.

He barked out a trite, "Let's save it for the field!" But it was obvious, even to him, that Nelson's reaction was far beyond anything mere football could arouse.

The big lineman snatched up a forty-five-pound plate from the weight rack and flung it at the wall. Crack! It took a three-inch chunk out of the cream cinder block.

Something must have told the coach that Nelson's mental state was not reachable by threats of benching or even expulsion from the team. Being an old linebacker, he dove forward, catching his lineman behind the knees, and toppling him to the floor. Even then it took six of us to hold him down.

"You're benched!" the coach bawled in his face. "And if I see another outburst like that, I'm calling the cops!" He clapped his hands. "Now, let's get out there."

We were afraid to let him up, but Nelson himself panted, "I'm cool! I'm cool!"

Todd and I lagged behind with him as the rest of the guys took the field.

Todd was brutal. "Way to go, nut-job! What

the hell was *that* supposed to be?"

To our absolute shock, tears began to stream down Nelson's cheeks. "Melissa's cheating on me!"

Todd blanched, but he recovered quickly. "Melissa? No way."

"I *know* it!" the lineman sputtered.

"It's impossible," Todd insisted. "That girl's totally into you."

"She has a hickey!" Nelson wailed. "On her—" He thought better of finishing that last sentence and added, "And I didn't give it to her!"

For me, it was like watching a bad dream coming true. My free-floating uneasiness about Jake's parties was starting to play itself out in real life.

Todd didn't blow his cool. "Dude, you were so wasted last night! You were all over Melissa. I saw you."

Nelson shook his head vehemently. "I don't forget stuff like that. Not with her. I can't play today," he added, forgetting the fact that he was benched anyway. "I can't face the field. To look up at the crowd and know that *he* could be out there somewhere—"

"He's not," I assured him with a loaded glare at Todd.

Nelson was angry. "How do you know, Rick? You don't even have a girlfriend. You don't know what it's like." He glared resentfully at Todd. "You neither. Didi would never cheat on you."

That hit Todd right where he lived. The fact was, Todd knew exactly what it was like.

Coach Hammer was standing at the end of the tunnel. "Come on, you three. Move it!"

Nelson pounded onto the field.

Todd grabbed my arm and held me back. "We're on the same page, right? Not a word to anybody, *ever!*"

"Right," I confirmed. It was true. I would never betray him. But it wasn't out of any sense of loyalty or obedience to the great Todd Buckley. What I'd seen in the locker room that day confirmed something I'd always believed: this was not just boys being boys. Nelson's pea brain was incapable of comprehending, let alone controlling, his arsenal of destructive power. And the emotional forces set in play by Jake's parties had put him over the edge.

I didn't intend to be responsible for his first murder.

If the front row had been filled with college scouts and not a phalanx of potbellied dads,

Todd would not have done himself much good that afternoon. Maybe it was his near miss with Nelson in the locker room; maybe it was the late Friday night at Jake's; or maybe it was just the simple fact that he wasn't all that good to begin with. None of us were. I can't believe we won.

Liberty wasn't great either, but they'd put together a decent record the season before. And none of their former coaches were doing time.

On the first series of the game, they marched effortlessly down the field and scored. It didn't bother us very much—we were used to stinking. But it practically killed Dipsy, who had established himself a few rows behind the visitors' bench. He had the section to himself and his popcorn and chips, because most of our fans knew to give him a pretty wide berth. There he sat, stuffing his face until it was time to cheer "RUN!" or "THROW!" or "HIT 'EM!"

"WHAT ARE YOU, REF—BLIND, STUPID, OR BOTH? THAT WAS %@&!$*# HOLDING!"

Perhaps I forgot to mention that in addition to a voice like a foghorn, Dipsy also had a mouth like a toilet.

The pathetic amount of resistance offered up by our defense on the opening drive convinced

Coach Hammer that he'd better unbench Nelson. So what if the guy had nearly converted our locker room to a pile of rubble? If all his anger could be chaneled into a tackle or two, it was worth the risk of putting him out among humans.

Todd sputtered. His timing was off, his accuracy was off, and he didn't throw a decent spiral all day. But after one of many punts by yours truly, Nelson, now anchoring the defense from the nose tackle spot, forced a fumble on our opponents' six-yard line.

With goal to go, our offense came in and gained negative seven yards. But that was still close enough for me to kick the field goal on a perfect snap from Jake: 7–3.

Remember, this was Jake snapping to Todd, the holder. So I was kind of impressed the ball hadn't been aimed at the guy's throat. The two had not spoken since the confrontation at the party the night before. But it was plain that, if they had ever been friends, they weren't anymore.

I did note that, at the opposite end of the bleachers from Dipsy's base of operations, Didi was wearing Todd's jersey. I had no idea what that was supposed to signify. Beside her,

Jennifer was fast asleep, a baseball cap pulled down to her chin.

Jake saw me looking in Didi's direction. "It doesn't mean anything," he assured me. "She's with me now." But I could tell it bugged him.

As the game progressed, Nelson's rage escalated. Every time Melissa and the cheerleaders took the field, he was reminded afresh of why he hated the world, and therefore Liberty. His tackles were train wrecks; his blocks cleared a path you could drive a truck through. Each bruising hit was made with such fury that I honestly started to feel sorry for the Lions.

I heard their coach exhorting his players, "Don't be afraid of that guy!" It was too much to ask. *We* were afraid of Nelson, and we were his teammates.

We still trailed 7–6 at halftime.

Considering we were only in this contest because of the wrath of Nelson Jaworski, the coach's pep talk was very subdued.

"Remember, it's only a game. We don't want anybody to get hurt."

Those burning effigies must have been of someone else's grandmothers.

It did nothing to slow Nelson down in the second half. Our offense stank, but their offense was completely neutralized by a rampaging lunatic. They didn't score another point. The most offensive thing that happened in the game's final stanza was that Dipsy emptied a two-pound bag of Chex Mix over the visitors' bench. In the ensuing shouting match, he was ejected from the stadium for calling the referee something that would grow hair on the palm of your hand.

This was not unexpected. Sooner or later, Dipsy was thrown out of every Broncos game. The fans awarded him a standing ovation as the back judge escorted him to the exit. In a way, it was the most respect poor Dipsy ever got at Fitz, and probably the main reason he had landed himself on the guest list for Jake's parties.

He was gone, but not forgotten. We could still hear his ranting from the parking lot.

To make a long and vicious story short and vicious, the game came down to a field goal attempt with six seconds to play. It was a moment that really would have appealed to the college scouts who never showed up.

As we got set for the kick, Todd decided to end his silent treatment of Jake. "Don't screw it up, Garrett! *Some* of us have college careers to think about!"

"Some of us should have thought of that before going oh-for-fifty!" Jake shot right back.

"Hey!" Todd leaped up from the holder's position, effectively scuttling down the attempt. "Who are you to criticize me? Coach hasn't got you busting your butt playing offense and defense and special teams like the rest of us! You want my advice? Keep on doing your little snaps and shut up, because pretty soon people are going to start wondering why you're so unique!"

I could feel the tide turning against Jake on the field. That speech really resonated with the exhausted players. One by one the linemen rose out of their stances to cast unfriendly looks in Jake's direction.

The whistle blew. "Delay of game!" bawled the ref. "Five yard penalty. Still fourth down."

I was grateful for the interruption. A few more seconds and some of our guys might have started shoving.

"Come on, Buckley!" shouted the coach from the sidelines. "What are you waiting for?"

All at once, people remembered we were in the middle of a football game—one that the Broncos might actually win. Snap, hold, and kick, and we came away with a 9–7 victory.

When the final score was announced over the loudspeaker, Dipsy charged back in from the parking lot, howling like a madman. He took out the Gatorade bucket with a flying tackle, showering our bench with an icy spray. In any other situation, he would have been burned at the stake. But there was something about winning that made everything okay.

Our fans felt it too. They stormed the field, encircling the victorious quarterback. Never mind that every single point had come off my foot.

Closer to the real truth was that Jake was the hero today. Last year, at least one of my field goals would have been blown because of a bad snap. Coach knew exactly what he was doing by letting Jake break his no-specialists rule.

I grabbed our long-snapper by the shoulder pads and steered him clear of the celebration. "You don't need to frolic with those idiots."

"Let go, baby." He squirmed free of me and wheeled to scan the surging crowd.

I could almost see him deflating when he spotted them—Todd and Didi, locked in a triumphant embrace at the center of the cheering throng.

"Sorry, Jake."

"She only does it out of pity." He never took his eyes off the sight of them. "She feels responsible for maintaining his *image*."

I kept my mouth shut. I was just now getting to know the real Didi Ray.

From what I could tell, she wasn't that self-sacrificing.

chapter
eleven

JUST AS JAKE'S parties had acquired an unpleasant taste, the tone at school was beginning to turn ugly. The buzz was still all about Jake—now that his long-snapping had lifted the pathetic Broncos to victory, he was more famous than ever. But the speculation about him had become suspicious, derisive. Jake had no longer dropped from heaven to provide high-quality Friday night entertainment; he was putting something over on us, playing us. And the mysterious attributes that had proved so irresistible before were simply more proof that the lowdown sneak was up to no good.

"I mean, he's a cool guy and all that," a junior girl was saying in the cafeteria on Monday. "But—"

This "but" was a telltale feature of several conversations I overheard that week. Jake was cool; Jake was great; he was fun. But.

"—but where does he get the money for such huge parties?" she finished.

"Well, obviously he's dealing drugs," replied one of her friends. "You don't make that kind of cash delivering the *Tribune*."

"You guys are missing the point," put in another girl. "The parties are a cover for the dealing. I've heard Jake's running a supermarket over there."

"I don't know." The first speaker was dubious. "I've been to a couple of those parties, and I never saw anything like that."

"Are you kidding?" the third girl crowed. "Babies could get born, and no one would ever notice at Jake's place."

It was interesting—I knew exactly where Jake's money was coming from, and it had nothing to do with drugs. But there were kids who swore up and down that they'd seen Jake selling X and loose joints in the upstairs hall.

And did anyone plan to skip the next bash to avoid being swept up in a narcotics sting operation? Not on your life.

"Those parties are the only excitement we've

got around here," said a tall red-haired boy in the food line.

Another weird thing: going by the buzz at Fitz, it seemed like everybody in school was a regular Friday night attendee. The parties were crowded, sure, but not with eighteen hundred people. Guys were speaking with authority on the layout of the Garrett home and the location of the best make-out spots. Most of them had to be lying, but the rumors were so wild anyway, it was hard to tell who. I think some kids were so wrapped up in Jake World that they almost believed they had been there—the way your mind can manufacture real memories of things your parents say you did as a young child.

As Jake's right-hand man, I picked up my share of piercing stares and dirty looks that week. Phil Braggett gave me a long lecture on the subject of my unwittingly "helping Jake screw us over."

I stuck up for Jake. "It's just a few parties. That's it."

"And you don't think it's weird that the guy came out of nowhere?"

"He didn't come out of nowhere," I explained patiently. "He went to a different school last year. He lives here now. And because he's new, he throws parties to get to know people."

"Well, I think he's a narc!" Phil spat out.

"A cop?"

"Working undercover as a student. It's a sting against underage drinking."

"And he hasn't found it yet?" I laughed. "That would make him the dumbest cop on the force."

Phil was undaunted. "Maybe he's biding his time, waiting to move in."

"Trust me," I assured him. "If Jake arrested every underage drinker he saw, this school would be empty. This is crazy, Phil."

He looked at me resentfully. "That's not what Todd said."

I was instantly alert. "Todd Buckley?"

But who else could he be talking about? Actually, it made perfect sense. Our great and exalted quarterback had soured on Jake. Therefore it was only a matter of time before everyone else fell into line. I love high school. It's a place for individuality to flourish.

I cornered Todd in the locker room before practice. "What have you been telling people about Jake?"

He scowled at me. "I knew you'd defend him."

"Defend him from what?" I exploded. "He hasn't done anything! The guy has a few parties, and you've got him ratting for the cops!"

"How do you know he isn't?" Todd shot back. "He appears out of thin air, and suddenly he's on the Broncos, he's throwing parties, he's all over school. Every toilet around here is stopped up with Jake Garrett! I've got the citywide college recruiting seminar tomorrow, and there'll be players there from McKinley. Maybe Jake did the same thing over there. I'm going to get to the bottom of this guy if it's the last thing I do."

"You know exactly what he's up to," I muttered bitterly. "That's what really bothers you, isn't it? You're the big expert when it comes to messing around with other people's girlfriends."

For a minute, I thought he might even take a swing at me. Instead, he fixed me with a snake-eyed glare. "Don't go there, Rick. You think you're hot stuff because you kick a few field goals, but let's see how popular you are if you get on my bad side."

I only saw Jake at practice, with Todd in the vicinity, so it was hard to get a sense of what the man himself thought of all this. Jake had become almost an automaton around the Broncos these days, performing his simple function, and staying out of everybody's way. But that was mostly because none of the other players talked to him anymore.

That's why, when I rounded the corner to my locker on Thursday and found myself staring into the depths of the Jake smile, I couldn't help grinning. I liked being Jake's best friend, and that didn't change with the tide of public opinion.

"Hey, baby—" He pumped my hand while gently but insistently guiding me away from my locker. "What do you say we ditch the afternoon? Call it a mental-health sabbatical."

I thought it over for about a nanosecond. With Todd, the center of Fitzgerald's football universe, away at the recruiting seminar, practice was probably going to be a joke anyway—just some basic drills and a ton of calisthenics. As for classes—

"I'm in," I agreed. "We should probably talk anyway. I'm sure you've noticed things with Todd are getting kind of nasty."

He seemed completely serene. "I'm not worried about him."

"Yeah, well, I am," I told him. "Todd's got a lot of clout around this place. He can make things pretty unpleasant for you if he sets his mind to it."

But Jake just led the way out to the Beamer in

the parking lot. He seemed to be in a fantastic mood.

I settled myself in the passenger seat. "Where to?"

"It's a surprise."

It did surprise me, although it shouldn't have. We cruised through the neighborhoods of Colonials, ranches, and splits that made up my mother's business universe until we pulled up at a gas station just out of sight of St. Mary's School for Girls.

Didi waited expectantly at the passenger door until I got out and sat down in the back. Jennifer crawled right over me and stretched luxuriously across the soft leather.

"You're on my half," I told her.

"I love you too, Ricky," she purred.

"Hey, ladies," beamed Jake, as Didi sidled over and began nibbling on his neck. "School burn down?"

The mere mention of school seemed to deflate Didi's passion. "Don't I wish," she grumbled, slumping in her seat.

"School can't be that bad," I goaded her. "You've got your old math tutor back, right?"

Jake cast a beseeching look over his shoulder. Apparently, not much tutoring had been going on during those long nights at the Garrett house.

We headed downtown to the small Greenwich Village–wannabe neighborhood that surrounded the Atlantica University campus. Cruising the main drag with the windows open, Jake exchanged greetings and the occasional high-five with the various research-paper customers we passed. Connor Danvers was one of them. To my surprise, he greeted Jake like a long-lost brother, risking life and limb to stand on the centerline to embrace the guy.

The subject of the late quantum physics paper never came up. "We're on for Friday night at your place, right?" Connor enthused. "Anything I should bring?"

"People," Jake said readily. "The more the merrier, baby."

"They're lining up to come," Connor assured him.

I tried to sound a cautious note. "If that lunatic invites the whole world, you'd better be shopping for a bigger house."

But I could tell that Jake was in his glory. He had Didi at his side, seeing him treated like a big shot—at a college campus, no less. It was working, too. Her look of rapturous admiration was too total to be faked. It was eerily similar to the expression she wore when playing her other Academy Award role of God's girlfriend.

Even Jennifer had no taste for discouraging words today. "Mellow out, Ricky."

We had a high-caffeine, high-sugar lunch of mochas and monster cookies at the Starbucks on the corner, and checked out a few stores. Jake and Didi kind of melted into each other as the tour progressed, until they could hardly move, epoxied laterally together in the style of a three-legged race.

"Those two should get a room," I whispered to Jennifer.

"Right now, I've got an afternoon off, and Jake has a BMW," was her reply. "So don't hassle it."

Eventually, we were back in the car, parking on a deserted dead-end street a bad punt from the dirty blue water of Lake Michigan. It was a make-out spot, no question about it. I glared at the back of Jake's head. Didn't he notice that his two rear passengers weren't dating?

In the front, Didi crawled over the gearshift console into Jake's lap. It was an awkward operation because of the position of the steering wheel, but she managed to make it look sexy because she was Didi. I rolled my eyes at Jennifer, who shrugged.

This isn't happening, I thought, trying to ignore the sounds coming from up there. It was a joke, right? Surely we weren't stuck here while those two did what came naturally.

A light fog began to materialize on the inside of the Beamer's windows. Jennifer reached over and traced out HELP with her finger. I grinned appreciatively and wrote: CONTENTS UNDER PRESSURE on my side.

All at once, she grabbed my hand. "Hey, Stud. Let's show these amateurs how it's done."

"Right, Warrior Princess." I jumped on her lap with an exaggerated moan. We overbalanced and keeled over sideways across the backseat in a symphony of manufactured slurping noises. The lovebirds gave no indication that they'd noticed. They wouldn't have noticed a mortar attack.

We forged ahead, determined to make our point. I hooked my foot over top of Didi's headrest, working up enough hyperventilation to erase the messages on the misted windows. Jennifer pulled off her scarf and tossed it over the front seat. In what I hoped was a vampire-like gesture, I buried my face in her neck and blew a loud raspberry. Laughing, she put her arms around my back and hung on.

"Behold, Princess—I hear the trumpet of

battle!" I declared, digging in for another blow.

I felt her fingers burrowing into my hair, pressing my lips against her skin too hard for bugling. "You're crushing the trumpet of battle," I said in a muffled voice.

That was when I noticed that Jennifer wasn't laughing anymore, or squirming to avoid my weight. The realization was a jagged fork of lightning that stretched from my head to a lower, less public part of my anatomy. What was the deal here? Was this a joke?

She wasn't joking—she was into it!

Or was she? This was Jennifer, after all.

I shrugged off the sting. Today, I'd find out one way or the other. Sure, I might make an idiot out of myself. Family friends—I'd never be able to escape the embarrassment. There could be no dignified retreat. Jennifer would become my Vietnam.

On the other hand, why should I be the only person who thought about consequences in this town? Nobody else ever did. Melissa cheated on Nelson; Todd cheated on Didi. Didi cheated on Todd. It was happening just a few feet in front of me—Jake and Didi, swapping tonsillectomies and God knows what else. Jennifer had the right idea: *It's all about me*. From this moment on, Rick Paradis did what felt good for Rick Paradis—starting in the backseat of the car that had replaced Jake Garrett's mother.

I maneuvered my mouth to Jennifer's . . . and froze.

The thrashing around behind the steering wheel had ceased abruptly, to be replaced by whispers—Jake's voice. It was garbled, but the phrase *break up with Todd* was unmistakably in there several times.

"Don't ruin it!" Didi hissed, louder than Jake.

I caught a meaningful glance from Jennifer; she was listening too. Whatever moment had been under construction between us, it was over. We were eavesdroppers now, ears at the keyhole.

Jake was speaking again, his persistence clear even though his low voice was not. Didi kept interrupting, "No! . . . No! . . . Shut up! . . ." until finally she rasped, "Why do you always have to spoil everything? Isn't it enough that I'm with you *now*?"

She was back in the passenger seat in a heartbeat. "We're going home." It wasn't a suggestion. It was a proclamation.

It took the Beamer's defoggers only a few seconds to erase all evidence of their passion.

chapter
twelve

OUR OPENING-DAY victory over Liberty convinced Coach Hammer that the key to our season lay in the kicking game. I practiced field goals until I thought my leg would fall off. My mouth worked even harder. With snapper Jake and holder Todd no longer talking to each other, I had to keep up a steady stream of peppy chatter to fill in all the hostile silences. And with those two, every moment was as silent as it was hostile.

Officially—or at least when anybody was watching—Didi seemed to belong to Todd. But I'd seen her VW in the neighborhood late at night. And judging from the undisguised loathing with which Todd and Jake regarded each other, I could tell that neither of them could figure out whose girlfriend she really was and why. I wondered if Didi herself knew.

I hadn't kicked from a tee all week, so I stuck around after Friday's workout for a few kickoffs. Most of the guys had already dressed and left by the time I hit the showers.

I was soaping up when I heard a loud crash, followed by full-throated yelling. I rinsed, clambered into jeans, and ran around to the chalktalk area. Big Nelson Jaworski had hold of Todd underneath the arms, the way you'd pick up a newborn baby. He was shaking our helpless quarterback like a rag doll, slamming him against a row of lockers.

"I trusted you!" Nelson roared. "I thought you were my friend! And it was you the whole time!"

"It wasn't—" Todd began feebly.

"Shut up!" Nelson hurled him into a rolling rack of footballs. The cart fell over, and Todd fell with it, hitting the concrete floor with the bouncing and wobbling balls.

"People saw you!" Nelson almost shrieked, and I could see how close to the edge he was. "You and Melissa ducking into Jake's bathroom! Even into one of the bedrooms!"

"No!"

"Nelson!" I shouted.

Don't get me wrong. I personally had no problem with Todd taking a beating over this. But Nelson was dangerous. In this state, he was like a little kid who had somehow gotten his hands on a pistol. Only here the weapon was two hundred sixty pounds of brute strength, powered by revenge-driven rage.

He noticed me for the first time. "Get out of here, Rick! This is between me and him!"

He picked Todd up by the scruff of the collar and reared back a fist the size of a Christmas ham. I took a running leap at him. He didn't even flinch when I jumped on his back. It was like striking something totally solid—a tree or a parked car. I grabbed his arm and held on for dear life. He howled with rage and flung me off. I hit the lockers face first and tasted blood.

Nelson wheeled his menace back on Todd, who had managed to scramble to his feet. More important, my side attack had provided our quarterback with the time he needed to come up with the story that might weasel him out of this mess.

"You've got it all wrong, man! I never touched Melissa!"

"Liar!" the burly lineman closed in for the kill.

Todd back-pedaled, stumbled on a football, righted himself. "I didn't want to say anything because we need him for the team. Nelson—it's Jake!"

"No!" I shouted through swelling lips.

Nelson hesitated. "I never saw Melissa with Jake."

"That's his whole style," our quarterback insisted. "That smooth 'Hey, baby, how's it going, baby?' He brings you to his house, fills you full of beer, treats you like his best friend. Then, when you're too buzzed to notice, he stabs you in the back."

"That's bull!" I snapped. "Jake barely knows Melissa!"

Todd's audience was Nelson, not me. "Think, Nelson! We had a good thing going. We had our girlfriends, played our ball. What's different? Who came out of nowhere and poisoned everything?"

"Jake." The big lineman's voice was uncertain. But I could see the wheels turning deep inside that thick skull of his.

"Don't listen to him," I said urgently. I was stuck. How could I get Jake off the hook without turning Nelson right back on Todd? "He doesn't know what he's talking about."

"It only happened once—last Friday night," Todd persisted. "While you were passed out. That's why I pulled her into that bedroom. I was trying to talk some sense into her. She wouldn't listen. Jake had her totally snowed." His expression was open and sincere. "Don't be too hard on Melissa. It was almost like Jake had her under some kind of spell."

"He's dead!" roared Nelson.

"No!" I jumped into his path. "You've got it all wrong! Jake would never do something like that—"

As soon as I said it, I felt ridiculous. Jake was doing *exactly* that to Todd, just like Todd was doing it to Nelson.

Nelson swatted me aside as he stormed to the clubhouse door. He turned to face us. "He's going to bleed. Tonight—at the party." And he was gone.

I shot Todd a furious glare. "I understand why you had to lie to save your neck. But why sic that maniac on poor Jake?"

"Poor Jake?" He practically spat it at me. "Do you know what Jake *really* is?"

"A good guy!" I shot back. "Who happens to have a thing for Didi, because *everybody* has a thing for Didi! And if you didn't treat her like bug crap, she wouldn't be looking for people to have things with!"

"Jake's nothing but a phony," Todd argued. "All the clothes, the parties, the 'Hey, baby'— that's not Jake. At the recruiting seminar I talked to some guys from McKinley—"

I cut him off. "I don't care how he was at McKinley. I only know Jake now—a friend."

"But it's a lie!" I'd never seen our quarterback so outraged. "He put one over on every kid at Fitz, me included! I was as fooled as the rest of you guys!"

If I hadn't been so agitated, I would have laughed right in his face. I mean, it was pretty much out in the open that his girlfriend had been cheating on him. And what did he choose to single out as the key injustice in the whole business? The fact that an outsider had broken the commandment against being as happening and popular as Todd Buckley.

"Look, I understand you're mad at the guy," I reasoned. "I would be too if I were you. But Nelson's a live grenade looking for a place to go off. We've got to find a way to call him back before somebody winds up in the hospital."

Todd shrugged. "Not my problem."

"It *is* your problem," I insisted. "Jake never touched Melissa. You did."

He regarded me sharply. "And Nelson's never going to find out about that, right Rick?"

"Don't push me," I warned. "If it comes down to you or Jake, I choose Jake. I'll rat you out."

"He's got you brainwashed! Just like Didi!"

"There's brainwashing here, all right," I shot back. "But it's not coming from Jake; it's coming from you. Everybody around here thinks you're something more than a third-rate quarterback at a third-rate school. And you're not! If I feed you to Nelson, the sun will still rise tomorrow."

He was choked with shock and rage. Nobody talked to Todd like this. "Not for you," he seethed, and stormed out of the locker room.

I knew exactly what he meant. To take sides with Jake against Todd Buckley would be a hanging offense at Fitz. I'd be an instant outcast.

A high-school leper.

By the time I got to Jake's place on the bus, Marty Rapaport was backing an ancient Chevy Suburban up to the Garrett garage.

"Where's Jake?" I barked in the window.

He favored me with a grin of recognition. "Hey, cross-bite, how's it hanging?"

Connor Danvers and a few other party veterans from Throckmorton Hall poured out of the hulking SUV and began unloading a procession of shiny kegs out of the back. I counted four of them.

"Jake bought all this?" I asked Marty.

"Some of it's mine," he admitted. "I invited a few friends to stop by tonight."

"A few?" I asked as the parade of heavy silver barrels entered the house via the back hallway. From a downstairs window next door, I caught a glimpse of Mrs. Appleford scowling at the beer and me.

"Several," he amended. "Jake said it's no problem."

"Well, it is a problem," I told him. "Because the party's off."

He laughed. "Sure, it is. Listen, a party like this—it's bigger than you and me. It's bigger than Jake. Trust me—it's happening."

"Jake!" I barged into the house.

He was in the living room, supervising the placement of the kegs into two ice-filled kiddie pools. "Hey, baby," he greeted when he saw me. "What do you think? Feed your racehorse an extra pail of oats so he won't fade in the stretch. This is going to be some party."

"Send them back," I told him. "You've got to cancel tonight." I filled him in on the locker-room altercation between Todd and Nelson.

Jake was grim but undeterred. "It's going to be me and Didi from now on," he said. "I'll have to face Todd sooner or later."

I stared at him. "Todd isn't the problem here. It's Nelson. The guy's got a screw loose anyway, and he's extra nuts now that he knows Melissa's been cheating on him."

"I'll be careful."

"You're not being careful!" I accused. "Nelson's a wild animal! You think anyone's going to sacrifice themselves by getting between you and him tonight? Definitely not Todd, or anybody who cares what Todd thinks, which is just about everybody."

"I'm not canceling the party," he said flatly. "I've come too far to turn back now."

"But you've already got Didi," I argued. "She's the grand prize, right? If she really likes you, that isn't going to change because you skipped one Friday night. And if all she cares about is your parties, who needs her, man?"

He hesitated. I realized that was the only way to get through to Jake. If you tried to reason with him, it went in one ear and out the other. The only way to get his attention was to structure your argument in terms of the sole currency of any value to him—wanting Didi, having Didi, keeping Didi.

I knew Jake liked me. But at a certain point our friendship was one-sided, because all he truly cared about was Didi.

At last, he managed to work up a careworn version of the Jake smile. "You're coming tonight, right, baby?"

"I can't keep Nelson off you."

"Not for that. It's going to be a major blowout! You have to be here."

The four kegs loomed like the cooling towers of a nuclear power plant. The word meltdown formed on my lips, but I didn't speak it aloud.

He looked at me hopefully, "Right, baby?"

I sighed. "Right."

I've often wondered if I did the right thing saying yes. I was his staunchest, and pretty much his only ally at Fitz. If I had refused to come that night, would it have been the 911 call that penetrated his laser-beam singleness of purpose? Would he have seen reason and called off the party?

At that moment, even Jake must have realized that something awful was about to happen.

chapter
thirteen

IT WAS AS if Jake was throwing a party in the
Twilight Zone. So much of it was familiar—the
house, obviously. Hundreds of revelers squeezed
into a small space, drinking tap beer out of plastic cups. But I didn't see a single solitary soul I
knew. It was strange—like turning on your
favorite TV show and finding the entire cast
gone, replaced by new actors. Yet the sets, the
props, the storylines—they were all the same.

Fully a third of the crowd must have been from
Throckmorton Hall and Atlantica University,
because they were older than the rest of us. One
guy looked about twenty-five and was wearing a
wedding ring, although that might have been a
gag for his big night slumming it with us high

school kids. But even without wedding rings, the college types were easy to spot—and not just because of their age. They were taller, but skinnier (dorm food?), and more of them smoked. A heavy cloud of stale tobacco stench hung just below the ceiling.

Their fashion statements were more extreme. At Fitz, a nose ring or a pierced tongue was front-page news. I spotted an A.U. girl with so much hardware hanging off her face that she could have caused an airport metal detector to self-destruct. Another wore her hair shaved down to quarter-inch length, with a spiderweb pattern razor-cut to her scalp. A few of the guys had so many tattoos that they reminded me of *The Illustrated Man*.

The high-school kids looked strange too, but only because I didn't know any of them. I felt like I was balancing on a precarious knife-edge of unease. On the one hand, the outsiders made me nervous; on the other, I wasn't so anxious to see a familiar face—if that face happened to belong to Nelson, let's say. A confrontation between that gorilla and Jake seemed inevitable, but I prayed that it wouldn't come tonight. Maybe Todd wouldn't show up either—fat chance. The king never missed an opportunity to make merry with his adoring subjects.

Marty Rapaport's extra kegs had ratcheted the alcohol consumption up to the next level. This was not social drinking, not even teenage party drinking. And it wasn't fun anymore, not even crazy fun. It was almost as if they could see the future—that this would be Jake's final Friday night, and the capital-P Party would be over soon.

I was happy to spot one of the regulars, Dipsy, next to some guys who were taking turns whacking each other about the head and shoulders with a Nerf lacrosse stick.

I greeted him like a long-lost brother. "Hey, Dipsy, do you know any of these people?"

"Thousands of species flock to the reef for its abundance of food and proximity to the sun's light," he replied between methodical bites of Pringles.

"Yeah, but are there any fish from Fitz on this reef?"

He pointed into the kitchen. It was jam-packed in there—they were virtually shoulder-to-shoulder—but I managed to catch a glimpse of the Jake smile through the forest of body parts.

As I began to wade into the crowd, Dipsy grabbed my wrist. "You okay, Rick? You look a little—wired."

"Trust me," I assured him. "We're the sanest ones here."

As I got closer to Jake, I spied Didi with him. I hardly recognized her at first. She was still awesome, of course—nothing was going to change that. But she seemed frazzled, over-burdened almost. She was drinking, too, which was unusual for her. Didi was the kind of girl who would park a beer in her hand as a style accessory, not a beverage.

But tonight she held onto the neck of a bottle of champagne like it was the throttle of a stunt plane. Her words weren't slurred, but she was speaking much too loudly for a subject this private.

"I'll break up with Todd when I want to break up with Todd. I decide who I break up with and when. How'd you like it if I broke up with *you*?"

Jake was practically groveling. "Shhh! Didi, don't talk like that!"

I tried to change direction to escape that pathetic scene, but the crowd had closed behind me, and I was in the kitchen, for better or worse.

"Rick! Over here, baby."

Jake grabbed me by the arm and dragged me past the Longest Tongue contest to join him and

Didi in front of the dishwasher. He continued to cling to me, his lifeline to a world where he still had some self-respect.

"Some night, huh?"

I wasn't going to lie to him this time. "I've got a bad feeling about these people, Jake. They're going to wreck your house."

He gave me his coolest gesture of dismissal. "Don't sweat it, baby. Everything's under control."

There was a cry of pain as the edge of a metal tape measure sliced into the soft flesh of one of the contestants' tongues.

"Is it?" I asked. "Maybe it is, but how would we know? Who *are* these people? Some of them aren't even kids!"

"Why are you being such a buzz-kill?" Didi asked petulantly.

Judging by the level of champagne in her bottle, it would take a lot more than my attitude to kill *her* buzz.

A soft lasso looped over my head, settled around my shoulders, and tightened. I looked down to find myself ensnared by a long rope of silk ties, knotted end to end. Turning, I grabbed the line and yanked hard.

With a squeal, Jennifer came stumbling out of the crowd and ran smack into me.

"Howdy," she boomed over a slight trace of a hiccup.

I waved the string of ties at Jake. "Maybe you should have put that lock on your *dad's* door."

The theft didn't bother him. He laughed out loud, completely unconcerned, because that was the way Didi liked him to be.

Jennifer looked wounded. "How do you know I didn't bring these ties from home?"

I could smell champagne on her breath too. But she, apparently, had finished off her whole bottle, or at least lost it somewhere.

"Okay, I didn't," she babbled on. "But I could've. That's your problem, Ricky. You don't trust people."

"Should I?" I wriggled out of the lariat, which fell to the slimy floor.

"Probably not," she admitted. "People are scum. All they care about is *sex, sex, sex*." And with that, she turned and walked away. I followed her, mostly because I couldn't let any conversation end with those three magic words. Out of the corner of my eye, I caught a glimpse of one of the Longest Tongue hopefuls trying to strangle his co-contestant with Mr. Garrett's ties.

I elbowed my way through the partygoers,

determined not to lose sight of Jennifer. The output of effort required to stay within range drove home the reality: I was pursuing her. I was *after* her. If there was still ambiguity in our relationship by the end of the night, it was not going to be for lack of trying. It was only then that I admitted to myself that our brief wrestling match in the Beamer Wednesday afternoon had been very much on my mind ever since.

The living room was a wild scene. The dancing was fevered, driven, the music so loud that the vibration of the bass had knocked crooked every single picture on the walls. At the kegs, a beer war was in progress. Intrepid soldiers were spraying each other from the taps, while their lieutenants kept the pumps going and the pressure up. Still others argued angrily that squandering this precious resource was a crime against humanity.

I could see some of the Fitz kids now. In fact, most of the regulars were here. They were just hard to spot among the hundreds of newcomers. Some of the Broncos had the curtains down and were tossing cheerleaders, hammock-style. Melissa was one of the tossees, but the men in her life, Nelson and Todd, were still nowhere to be found.

I'd almost caught up to Jennifer. Reaching ahead, I grabbed her by the arm and spun her around. If she was surprised to see me tailing her, she didn't show it. Without missing a beat, she pulled me onto the dance floor, which was easy, because everywhere was sort of the dance floor. I did my best to gyrate along with the tight crush of people, but my attention kept wandering to the picture window over Jennifer's shoulder.

Out on the street, hundreds of headlights just hung there, unmoving. As packed as the party was, things were going to get worse. These were potential guests, waiting for parking spaces to open up. It occurred to me that if anybody left this house and drove away, there was going to be a fifty-car pileup out there as the whole world pounced simultaneously on the single open spot.

Jennifer frowned. "What are you looking at, Ricky?"

I was transfixed by a single headlight, growing steadily larger and brighter. It was an illogical thought, but the image that appeared in my mind was an express train, bearing down at top speed, about to flatten the Garrett house.

The roar of machinery drowned out the music—something I would not have believed possible. The door burst open, sending pieces of the lock and frame skittering across the floor. A big Harley exploded into the front hall. Kids dove out of its path, the contents of their drinks sloshing in all directions. The driver swerved left to avoid a tall rubber tree plant, and lost what little control he had. He went flying, and the chopper, now on its side, skidded across the tile floor and crashed into the newel post at the bottom of the stairs.

I wasn't exactly sure how I got there, because I don't remember running. Most likely, I was carried by the tide of people rushing to see if the driver was dead.

He wasn't. He shook off his helmet to reveal shoulder-length blond hair, bloody nose, and rapidly swelling lips.

I was the only person with the brains to reach over and turn off the Harley's motor before the carbon monoxide killed every single one of us. The roar sputtered and died just in time for us to hear the guy's "explanation" of what had happened:

"There's no place to park out there!"

Oh, that was reasonable. If you can't find a spot, your only alternative is to drive your motorcycle up the front walk, through a closed door, and into a roomful of innocent bystanders.

I waited for the crowd to fall on the driver and beat his stupid head in. Instead, they acted like it all made sense to them. A bunch of kids hauled him to his feet, dusted him off, and escorted him to join the chaos. He went, too, without so much as a casual glance at his disabled Harley, its ruptured tank leaking gas all over the tile floor.

Well, that was just peachy. A houseful of smokers and a big puddle of gasoline.

"Hey!" I called to the dispersing group. "We've got to clean this up!"

Jennifer looked at me as if I'd just suggested she dredge the harbor. "It's not my bike," she shrugged.

I dipped two fingers in the spill and held them up to her nose. "Take a whiff."

She sniffed and wrinkled her nose. "Seagram's?"

"Exxon! It's gas! One spark could put us all on the moon!"

She thought that was hilarious. But when I grabbed the roll of paper towels from the pizza table, she accepted a few sheets and went to work alongside me.

We scrubbed and sopped until we ran out

of towels. We finished the job with a couple of rolls of toilet tissue from the bathroom where Todd and Melissa had first begun the extra-curricular activity that was probably going to bring us all down, and soon.

I watched in horror as Jennifer started to cram the gas-soaked paper into an overstuffed garbage can.

"No!" I exclaimed, digging out an armful. "Someone could toss a lit cigarette in there!"

I looked around. The place was a mob scene. It wasn't exactly ideal for HAZMAT disposal.

I headed for the open front door. There were almost as many people out there as in the house. Points of light hovered about like orange fire-flies—glowing cigarettes, each one a potential explosion. They fluttered all over the lawn. No way could we dump the stuff outside.

"I know," said Jennifer, who was treating this whole thing like it was some kind of parlor game—Flammable Pictionary. "Let's flush it down the toilet."

"Are you going to pay Jake's Roto-Rooter bill?"

But she had a point. The only safe way was to get the gas-soaked paper in water.

My eyes fell on Budweiser Central—the four

gleaming kegs and, more important, the two wading pools full of ice cubes and slush. Perfect.

It took a few trips, but pretty soon we had all the towels and tissue in the melted water around the silver canisters.

"Hey, cross-bite, what are you doing to my property?" Marty Rapaport lurched over, his arm around the waist of one of the stars of the girls' volleyball team.

Shouting to be heard over the music, I explained about the motorcycle crash and the gas cleanup.

He brayed a laugh right in my face. "You two better get in there with it. You smell like a Mobil station."

I gave my sleeve a sniff. He was right. One spark, and I was cremated. Jennifer had the same problem.

"We'd better wash up," I decided.

The downstairs bathroom was locked tight as a drum. From the inside, you could hear the most horrible groaning and retching.

"Technicolor yawn," Jennifer reported. "We'll have to go upstairs."

Navigating the staircase wasn't easy. There were Slinky races in progress, and the betting was heavy. When I accidentally knocked one off course with my foot, I thought the owner was going to kill me. It took three of his friends to wrestle him to the floor, which was the only way to hold him back from throwing a punch at my face. Jennifer made a point of grinding her heel into his hand as we passed by.

We were lucky enough to catch the second-floor bathroom open. We slipped in and locked the door behind us.

I wet a washcloth and started sponging at the front of my shirt. I looked down and noticed that Jennifer was doing the same—only *her sweater was spread out on the bathmat!*

I dropped the cloth. At that moment, I wouldn't have noticed if my shirt was soaked with sulphuric acid that was eating my flesh down to the bone. The cleanup operation, for all intents and purposes, was over.

As turned on as I was, I didn't have the guts to make the first move. Instead, I stood there, waiting for her to notice me noticing her.

She kept on sponging, pretending this was a regular occurrence, and that she socialized in a black lace bra all the time.

And then I was down there with her. To this day, I couldn't tell you how I got there. It's entirely possible that I fell.

But the timing was perfect. I rolled to her, she rolled to me, and that was the start of a whole lot of rolling.

My lips, still swollen from their collision with a row of lockers, stung as I kissed her. I didn't care. I pressed my mouth to hers, grooving on the pain—confirmation that we were close and getting closer. My head banged against the side of the bathtub. Her elbow knocked over the laundry hamper. My mother, the real estate agent who sold this house, obviously knew nothing about the dimensions required for good maneuverability.

"Ricky, you're such an idiot," she murmured in my ear. "What the hell took you so long?"

I never knew being insulted could be so sexy. Jennifer and Rick, thrown together since forever, explored each other for the first time. And every touch, every sensation was supercharged with seventeen years of anticipation.

Funny, at this most adult of moments between me and her, I sank into a flashback that carried me to her sixth birthday party, eleven years before. We had played Pin the Tail on the Labrador retriever—Jennifer didn't like donkeys. And when it was time to go home, I was the last to leave. I remember being so proud about that.

It marked me as special. I got to stick around while Jennifer took an inventory of all her loot. There was one present—some kind of Barbie doll, the one with the surfboard. She didn't even open the package before tossing it disdainfully into the wastebasket.

"What did you do that for?"

"Liam gave the same Barbie to Kelsey two weeks ago," she said righteously.

"So?" I knew nothing about dolls. "Maybe it's a good one."

"If he wants to come to my party, he can't give me the same thing he gives everybody else!"

I had to hand it to her. She was tough. Even at age six.

At the time, though, I was mystified. "But why?"

"Because it's all about me."

Wait a minute. She couldn't have said that. Not then . . .

The flashback popped with a peal of laughter from Jennifer—today's Jennifer.

"What?" I murmured. Maybe I was short on technique, but no one ever laughed.

"Look!"

I followed her gaze to the overturned laundry

hamper. Among the tumbled boxers and sweat socks lay a white T-shirt, size Jake. On the front was written: MATHLETES DO IT BY THE NUMBERS, and in smaller letters: MCKINLEY MATH TEAM, 2001.

"I guess Jake needs another deadbolt," I mumbled, and reached for her again.

"Nerd alert!" she giggled.

"It's his shirt, Jen, not his mission statement."

"No, really," she insisted, her hot breath tickling my ear. "Didi told me. She finally 'fessed up. That's why she never gave Jake the time of day at McKinley. The guy was a wedgie looking for a place to happen."

"Give me a break—" But even as I protested, the pieces were coming together in my mind. The honors classes, college papers, chess trophy, math tutor . . .

"It's not so crazy, you know," she reasoned. "Around her friends, Didi had an image to maintain—prom queen, supermodel, who's who in *Who's Who*. But in front of Jake, who was nobody, she could be herself."

"And she started to like him," I concluded.

"He was the only person she could really talk to."

"How long did they go out for?"

She glared at me, exasperated. "They went out

for zero, that's how long. This wasn't the Jake you and I know."

"She liked him," I persisted.

"Look," she said. "Cool people can have uncool friends, and it's fine so long as they don't expect to get invited to the same parties, and hang with the same crowd, and date the same level of person. Jake was sweet, but life isn't *Revenge of the Nerds*. She hadn't thought twice about the guy until two weeks ago."

No wonder Jake was so mixed up. Always thinking he had to buy my friendship with fancy lunches or catered breakfasts; feeling he had to have something to offer, like just being himself wasn't enough. It certainly hadn't been enough for Didi Ray.

"Kind of lousy," I mumbled.

"What was she supposed to do?" Jennifer argued. "Chuck everything for her math tutor? He had potential, sure. But Didi's never been much of a creative thinker. Caterpillars aren't her type. She'll only go for a finished butterfly."

"Maybe life is *Revenge of the Nerds*," I said thoughtfully.

She nodded. "He almost pulled it off. But he couldn't keep his mouth shut—bugging Didi to dump Todd. Like that's ever going to happen!"

She climbed over me, straddling my chest to look straight down into my eyes. "Poor Jake. The whole thing's so pathetic, I almost care."

That ended it. If she'd offered up a truckload of gold bars along with herself, I still would have said no.

The decision brought seventeen years of gradually building sexual tension down to earth with a dull thud. Don't get me wrong—I didn't owe it to Jake. If the tables were turned, he would have sold my soul to the devil for five more minutes with Didi. I almost understood it, too. After what had happened to that poor guy two years before, it was easy to see how Didi was more than a girlfriend to him.

She was the ultimate affirmation, a megaphone blaring: *I'm as good as you! Don't I have the girl of everybody's fantasies right here in my arms?* It must have been enough to erase years of teasing that had surely been directed at an exceptionally bright kid.

"Way to go, Jake," I said aloud.

Jennifer frowned. "What's that supposed to mean?"

My departure was slowed by the fact that I was half dressed and on the bottom. I climbed out from beneath her, buttoning my shirt.

She was mystified. "Ricky, what's wrong?"

I could have, and probably should have told her that she was under Jake's roof, buzzed on his champagne, stuffed with his pizza, and fooling around on his real estate while bad-mouthing him. But if she had to ask, she didn't deserve the explanation.

She was getting angry now, covering herself up with her damp sweater. "What is your problem?" she snapped.

"You were right the first time," I told her. "It's all about you."

I walked out, slamming the bathroom door behind me.

chapter
fourteen

I WENT DOWNSTAIRS to find the party careening along at an appalling pace. The noise was up to the point of pain, and looking down from above, I couldn't spot one inch of floor. It was wall-to-wall people. At the foot of the stairs lay the motorcycle, now a piece of the Garrett house's topography. Everyone accepted it as they would the living-room couch. There was even a guy using one of the mirrors as a cup-holder.

The decision to go home was already set in my mind. I reversed myself, though, when I saw Todd Buckley slip in the broken door. There was no way I could leave without giving Jake a heads-up that there was trouble brewing. But before I could begin what was looking like an impossible search, Todd went into action.

He strode to the center of the living room. It was something to see how the crowd parted to let him through. I knew the Fitz kids would make way for royalty, but how did Throckmorton Hall and all these strangers know this was the great Todd Buckley?

Maybe he just had an air of command, because he went where he pleased, right up to the stereo, and yanked out the plug. The sudden quiet was as jarring as a bomb blast. All conversation ground to a halt. Jake's house, this boiler factory, this cacophony, was as silent as a tomb.

"*Garrett!*" Todd bellowed. "Get in here, Garrett! I've got something to say to you!"

There were a few wisecracks from the college kids, but they petered out in a hurry. It was pretty plain that whatever was happening, it was dead serious. I noticed a few of the Broncos shuffling closer to be near their captain at his big moment.

"*Gar-rett!*"

"Right here."

Our host entered from the hall that led to the laundry room. I was surprised to see the Jake smile on his face—and not a fake one, either. Maybe it was because he had Didi by his side, and that was all he'd ever wanted or cared about. A face-off with Todd had always been a part of the deal. He was ready, even happy to do this, if it put him a step closer to her.

It's hard to explain, but I was proud of him right then. Every fold of his J. Crew cottons was perfect, even though he had to squeeze through the sweat-soaked crowd to make his appearance. He didn't have a hair out of place, and his lithe, graceful gait reminded me of the first time I'd met him in this very room three weeks before. Back then I'd remarked on his poise under pressure. After all that had happened, now I was thinking, that goes double for tonight.

I began to push my way through the clammy bodies.

Marty Rapaport grabbed me and held back my progress. "Hey, cross-bite, what's going on? What is this, the O.K. Corral?"

I heard Jake's greeting to Todd. "Glad you could make it, baby. What's up?"

For a second there, I toyed with the possibility that he could brazen it through, that his sheer faith in who he'd become might do the job for him. This wasn't the old Jacob Garrett. This was Jake, reinvented. But as soon as Todd started talking, I knew the battle was lost.

"When I was at the recruiting seminar, I ran into some old friends of yours from McKinley, Jake—or should I say Jacob? Funny thing—the Jake Garrett they remember is a lot different from you. They told me about a nerdy little shrimp with giant glasses on his snot nose and a protractor sticking out of his butt."

Jake's voice remained calm, but his face was reddening. "I don't know what you're talking about."

"Maybe that's because you spent so much time stuffed into your locker by people who were sick of hearing about your science-fair projects and math trophies," Todd sneered. "And don't forget the chess club—you practically owned it, didn't you? Answer me this—how come a total loser at McKinley is suddenly all that at Fitz?"

Jake tried to stem the onslaught. "Listen, baby—"

"Because you're a lying piece of crap!" Todd roared in his face. "Something like this doesn't happen by accident! You think just because we aren't math geeks like you that we're too stupid to see what you've done to us?"

It went on, growing shriller and uglier by degrees. Todd sounded more like a prosecutor than an angry guy at a party. He was revealing evidence, presenting arguments, asking the jury to throw the book at this outlaw.

Marty looked at me. "He's kidding, right?"

To my eyes and sinking heart, nobody was kidding. The Fitz kids in the living room sported expressions that were close to triumphant. *By God, we knew there was something not quite right about Jake Garrett! We suspected it all along! We're mad as hell, and we're not going to take it anymore!*

Marty, who I didn't even like, seemed to be the only other person who understood how insane this was. "He got contact lenses, bought some new clothes, threw parties, and wrote a bunch of essays so he could afford to do it. What's so bad about that?"

Jake just stood there and took it, flushed but composed. I could see Didi, with carefully measured sidesteps, inching away from him.

"I may not be Einstein like you," Todd finished. "But I'm smart enough to know when I've been had. Did you honestly think you could get away with it?"

I found my voice at last. "Hey—"

That was all the speech I got to make. In through what was left of the front door stormed two hundred sixty pounds of Nelson Jaworski.

He looked as if he had spent the past several hours stoking his jealous rage into a white-hot homicidal one—which meant he fit perfectly into this place. And when he opened his mouth, his howl seemed barely human.

"Where's Garrett?"

Frantic, I started to push toward Jake. There had to be some way to smuggle him out of there under cover of chaos. Tomorrow, Mr. Garrett might come home to find his house in ruins, but at least his son would still be alive to try to explain it to him.

"Nelson!" Melissa tried to calm her boyfriend down, but her presence only reminded him of what he was so mad about.

In the middle of all this, a great laughing cheer was heard. Kendrick Jones and a few other Broncos exploded up the basement stairs, completely unaware of the drama unfolding on the main level. They held between them a huge Fourth of July skyrocket. I squinted at the object tied onto the back—a pair of jeans, legs dangling.

Dipsy came waddling up behind them, pantless as usual. "Aw, come on, guys, don't do this to me!"

But the group aimed the big firework straight

out the open front door, determined to put Dipsy's Levi's into orbit.

"Who's got the lighter?"

"I thought *you* had the lighter!"

That exchange was interrupted by the primordial shriek that came from Nelson as he spotted Jake in the crowd.

I called out a warning. "Run, Jake!"

Todd's fist came out of nowhere, connecting hard with my jaw. Reeling in shock and pain, I weighed my desire to hit back against the need to help Jake. "Run, man!" But even as I said it, I realized that, in this crowd, there was nowhere to go.

Nelson, on the other hand, had no problem getting around. People either got out of his way, or he flattened them.

Jake tried to make a break for the kitchen, but Nelson was upon him in three monster strides.

"I got it!" Kendrick held up a disposable lighter and raised the flame to the rocket's wick.

"No!" wailed Dipsy.

I watched in terror as Nelson reached out and grabbed Jake by the throat. And that's not just a figure of speech. I could see the lineman's huge hand completely encircling Jake's slender neck.

"Hey!" cried Marty. Even Todd blanched.

What happened next took place in the space of a split second, yet I remember it as a quick-cut action sequence in a movie—the shower scene in *Psycho*. Jake's eyes bulged in horror as his face began to turn a sickly gray-blue. Didi sprang over, and as she moved, she raised the champagne bottle she'd been hugging all night. Then, with a snap of her impossibly delicate wrist, she brought the bottle down on Nelson's head. It shattered. The big lineman dropped like a stone, releasing Jake, who tumbled free.

A loud crackle cut the air as the skyrocket's wick burned to the powder cache. At that moment, Dipsy made one last lunge for his jeans, and managed to get a grip on the left leg. Kendrick shoved him off, and in so doing, swung the firework away from the door until it pointed straight into the living room.

Hot sparks shot out of the back. With a cry of pain, Dipsy jumped away, relinquishing his grip. Then, in the language of NASA, we achieved liftoff.

You know how real rockets seem to start off slow, picking up acceleration with altitude? Well, this thing was the opposite of that. It shot across the room like it had been fired out of a cannon, clearing the crowd by inches. Kids threw themselves to the floor in a bruising pile-up of elbows, knees, and heads.

The big firework sizzled horizontally, then curved upward and slammed into the living-room ceiling. Instead of exploding, it came apart on impact, raining sparks, powder, and burning bits of cardboard over the two wading pools.

There was instant combustion. I gawked. The water was on fire!

That doesn't happen, I thought numbly, slapping at a smoldering spot on a lampshade. That's scientifically impossible.

Marty had a theory. "What's going on? Did somebody put booze in that water?"

"No!" That was when it hit me. Not booze; gasoline! The gas from the Harley must have separated from the paper towels. And gas floats on water!

Coughs and wheezes rang out as the blizzard of airborne powder found its way up noses and down throats. But most of the stuff settled gently over the flames where it ignited into an incandescent display of exploding red, white, and blue. The smells of smoke and sulphur filled the living room.

Just when I thought it was over, I heard a loud but persistent hiss. I stared. The flames had melted the skin of the plastic wading pools. As they slowly deflated, ponds of slush topped with burning gasoline spilled out onto the floor. Flaming streams snaked their way among party guests and overturned furniture.

"Run!" bellowed somebody, but the command was unnecessary. Hundreds of kids stampeded for the door, tripping over debris and each other. They came from everywhere—upstairs, the basement, the laundry room. Cries of "Fire!" and "The house is burning down!" rang out in the groundswell of panic.

The fact that ninety percent of these people had been drinking for several hours did not make for an orderly evacuation. Kids were stumbling on the steps, wiping out themselves and others. One of the Illustrated Men from Throckmorton spotted the flaming trickle below, declared "Lava!" and promptly fell down the stairs, taking a dozen others with him. He had to be physically dragged out of the house, babbling volcanic warnings.

I was about to abandon house myself when my eyes fell on Jake, stumbling around in the smoke and confusion. He looked frantic, which was pretty much the way you'd expect a guy to look when his house was on fire. What he didn't look like was someone who was leaving.

I ran over and grabbed his arm. "Come on! We've got to get out of here!"

He wheeled to face me, eyes blazing. "Where's Didi?"

"Outside!" I told him.

"Are you sure?"

"Yeah, I'm sure!" I wasn't, really. But I couldn't see her in the house. And if experience had taught me anything, it was that Didi generally looked after number one.

"I can't leave without her!" he persisted.

Once again, the extent of his pathological devotion boggled my mind. His carefully created world was quite literally coming down around his ears. His house was filling up with smoke. Whatever happened, this was not something he was going to be able to clean up with a mop and a few garbage bags. And what was his main concern? Didi.

This wasn't a crush. It wasn't even true love. It was total obsession.

I took advantage of the one piece of leverage I still had with the guy—I was bigger than he was. I dragged him out of there.

The front yard resembled the scene of an outdoor rock concert minus the Porta Pottis.

Some clusters of kids had actually staked out spots on the lawn where they could sit cross-legged to watch the "show"—presumably, the spectacle of Jake's side-hall Colonial burning to the ground.

I looked beyond the chaos to see two uniformed police officers racing across the grass toward us. For a moment, I couldn't figure out how they had responded so fast. Then I saw Mrs. Appleford, wrapped in the pink chenille bathrobe she wore twenty-four/seven, hovering on the property line. The neighborhood KGB had finally run out of patience for Jake's parties. She had complained to the cops just in time for the apocalypse.

"Call the fire department!" I yelled at them.

Distant sirens told me that this had already been done.

The officer in the lead pointed to the smoke billowing out the front door. "Is anybody in there?"

"No!" I shouted back. Then, "I don't think so." But how could I be sure there wasn't some drunk curled up in the basement, fast asleep? "I don't know!"

They bulled through the crowd and ran into the house. I could hear them crashing around inside. There was cursing as I think one of them tripped over the Harley.

"Over here, Lenny!" rang out loud and clear. "We've got a kid down in the living room!"

Desperately, I scanned the crowd. There was Todd, with an arm around Didi and the other holding Jennifer. Marty huddled with some of the college guys. Dipsy was flailing his jeans against a hedge in a desperate attempt to put out a small fire in the seat. Not far away milled his tormentors from the Broncos, chastened and sheepish, hoping no one remembered who it was that had set off a skyrocket in a private home.

I gave up looking. There were hundreds of strangers at this party. The person in there could have been anybody.

The cop ended the mystery with a single comment: "Give me a hand, will you? This guy weighs a ton!"

Nelson!

The big lineman hadn't moved since Didi had crowned him with that champagne bottle. If it wasn't for the cops, he would have been left to burn with the house.

I guess it had never occurred to me that he might be really hurt. This was Nelson Jaworski.

You couldn't hurt him with an atomic bomb. He did all the hurting.

But when they carried him out, the raucous crowd grew deathly quiet. His short curly hair was matted with blood, and he was obviously deeply unconscious.

The younger officer was shouting into his walkie-talkie. "We need an ambulance here now! Head wound, possible skull fracture, maybe smoke inhalation—this kid's in trouble!"

All that was plain as day, yet hearing the words out loud—cop-show words when this was real life—brought a fuzzy party world into jarring razor-sharp focus.

The older officer cupped his hands to his mouth and addressed the crowd in a foghorn voice: "Who saw what happened?"

There was total silence—an uneasy silence, although dozens of people must have been looking on when Didi swung that bottle.

"Come on," the officer prodded. "He didn't fall on the top of his head. Somebody hit him. Who did it?"

This officer had obviously never dealt with high-school kids before, because he was going about this in the worst possible way. The natural aversion to being a rat was almost primal, dating back to the first moment your mom told you, "Don't be a tattletale."

I could feel the crowd's resistance stiffening.

"You think this is a game?" The cop was getting angry. "This is a felony investigation! You want me to call for back up and bring fifty Breathalyzers? Tow all these cars, maybe?"

Jake was right beside me, so he saw what I saw—Didi, pale and shaking behind Todd. For an instant, I could read my friend's mind. I knew what he was about to do, but I couldn't stop him. I even reached for him, but he had already stepped forward.

"I did it."

To this day, I blame myself for not reacting faster. But in a million years I didn't think the confession would hold up. It was such a transparent half-assed attempt at chivalry. Surely someone would vouch for the guy who was being choked half to death at the time! Surely Didi would! If she cared enough about Jake to stop Nelson from strangling him, why would she let him hang himself for something he didn't do?

A small sigh, almost a moan, rippled through the crowd. Nobody said a word, least of all Didi.

That left me.

"It's not true! Jake, what are you doing, man?"

But the look of zealous determination on the face of Jake Garrett was one that I recognized all too well. It was the calculated driven fervor that had turned a lowly math tutor into a football player, a fashion statement, a legendary host, and a popularity machine—all to catch the eye of one girl.

Jake spoke up again, louder this time.

"It was me."

chapter
fifteen

THE GARRETT HOUSE didn't burn down that night. According to the papers, when the fire had worked through all the gas, there was too much water around for the flames to spread to anything else. Jake's wading pools had saved the day. It's a good thing we don't drink warm beer in this country.

In the end, the cops turned a blind eye to several hundred cases of disturbing the peace and underage drinking. They made only one arrest. Jake was led away in handcuffs. The charge: Assault with a dangerous instrument, with intent to cause serious physical injury.

I couldn't escape the feeling that, if I'd said something a little more quickly, I could have created enough doubt for them to leave him alone. On the other hand, at least the county lockup gave him a place to sleep that wasn't full of smoke.

The Garrett house was sealed off with police-line tape. It was the one thing that brought a trace of a smile to my lips in the terrible days that followed—the thought that Mrs. Appleford, self-appointed guardian of the neighborhood property values, now lived next door to a crime scene.

I could only imagine the phone call that had taken place between Jake in custody and Mr. Garrett in his hotel in Pocatello, Idaho. At that point, it would have been too late to get on a plane. So the father, I'm sure, passed a night not much more comfortable than the one endured by his son.

Mr. Garrett finally hit town at about the same time as Nelson Jaworski's eyes fluttered open at Mercy Hospital. The news was not great. Nelson had sustained a depression skull fracture. He would recover, but there might be permanent side effects. For one thing, he had no memory of the entire evening. This meant even he couldn't tell who had hit him or, more to the point, who hadn't.

But short-term memory loss, the doctors said, could be a sign of brain damage. Personally, I'd always felt that Nelson was pretty much brain-damaged long before he got hit. If that sounds callous, then tough. I would have had a lot more sympathy for Nelson if my last sight of him hadn't been with his hands around Jake's neck, trying to squeeze the life out of the guy.

I was never a fan of Didi's nonphysical attributes, but the fact was she had probably saved Jake's life—that was the most frustrating part. There was no crime here, unless you count the one that Nelson had been trying to commit. All Didi would have had to do was own up, explain the circumstances, and the whole thing would have been over. But at this point, coming forward would have seemed too convenient, inviting questions such as: Why the silence up till now? Had it taken her this long to cook up an excuse to get her friend off the hook? The stupid girl had converted a win-win into a lose-lose. And the big loser was going to be Jake, not her.

Air fresheners sat on every available surface in the Garrett house, but the smell of smoke was plainly evident. It mingled sickeningly with the heavy floral scent.

Jake was in deep trouble. He'd even been kicked out of school, pending his court hearing, since his crime involved an attack on a student. I didn't know what the future held for him, but I couldn't see it being anything good.

And what were his first words to me?

"Thanks for coming, baby. What do you hear from Didi? How's she holding up under all this?"

"To be honest, Jake, I haven't talked to her. She's got Todd running interference."

He nodded slowly. "I keep calling, but her folks won't put her on. I guess suspicion would fall on her if she talked to me."

I was burning. "Suspicion *should* fall on her! She did it! It's probably the only thing she did in her life that was for somebody else, but she did it!"

He just sighed. "Poor Didi."

"Poor Didi?" I repeated. "You'd better start thinking about poor Jake! That girl's going to let you take the rap for this! Think about it—what kind of person are you protecting? You've got to tell the truth and save yourself!"

"I couldn't do that to her."

"Why not?" I ranted. "She has no problem doing it to you!"

He acted as if he hadn't heard. "I just wish there was some way I could make sure she's all right."

"She's fine!" I exploded. "She's with Todd! She was always with Todd, and she's always going to be with Todd! And if she breaks up with Todd, she's going to find somebody exactly like Todd and be with him! She may have a fling every now and then, but the Didis of this world stay with their own kind!"

I'd never seen him look so wounded. The guy was practically under house arrest, a few days away from being charged with a felony, but that barely even registered in his thick skull. All that mattered was Didi.

I wouldn't leave. I was determined to stay until I could convince Jake to come clean. Even when he was called to the phone to talk with his lawyer, I stayed in his room, pacing like a caged tiger, wracking my brain for some new strategy that would make him see reason.

The closet door was partially open, and a large carton, loaded with stuff, sat on the floor. Curious, I peered inside. Science fair trophies and prize ribbons were piled on top of each other. A certificate signed by the mayor proclaimed Jacob Garrett to be the "2001 Mathlete of the Year." There were books about chess and Dungeons and Dragons, and pennants from Quiz Bowl and Odyssey of the Mind.

So it was true.

Underneath all that, I found mail-order catalogs from Abercrombie and Fitch, Banana Republic, Nike, Ralph Lauren, and J. Crew. There was also a well-thumbed paperback entitled *Understanding Football*, and, at the very bottom, a county real-estate map, with the school district divisions marked in red.

Jake stepped back into the room. "Sorry, ba—"

He froze when he saw me there, buried up to my waist in his secret history.

I stood, regarding him as if for the first time. "It was all for Didi, wasn't it? From the very beginning. You threw those parties just because you knew that Didi would eventually show up at one of them."

The pained expression on his face told me plainly that it went a lot further than that.

"You needed football to attract the right crowd, so you turned yourself into Coach's long-snapper. That was all about Didi too. You even *moved* here for her. You *planned* this—starting the very day she blew you off sophomore year."

He didn't deny it. His intensity was almost scary. "Do you know how it feels when the girl you love—who you know could love you—won't even look at you when she passes you in the hall because you're not cool enough? Because she doesn't want to admit to her friends that she even knows you?"

It occurred to me that he would never see the reality of what was being done to him. Because then he'd have to admit to himself that he'd been nothing more than an unimportant footnote in Didi's book. And that would mean accepting the fact that the last two years of his life had been totally meaningless.

How could you save a guy who wouldn't let himself be saved?

I didn't get a wink of sleep that night. Every time I closed my eyes, I had a vision of Jake, crouched in his backyard all summer in the broiling heat, long-snapping footballs at a target, or maybe an old tire against the side of the house. In my dream, he was drenched with sweat, his spine aching from the unnatural position, the back of his neck roasted and blistering in the sun. Every few snaps, he'd have to chase down his footballs and start the whole process over again. It was the kind of torture that took an iron will to overcome—especially since he had no interest in the game, never had, and probably never would. But there, hovering just above the heat shimmer, was Didi's face. And making the team brought him a step closer to her, so he plodded on.

I pictured him poring over those catalogs, staring at the models in J. Crew and Banana Republic, piecing together a look for the new Jake, formerly Jacob, that would catch her eye and win her heart. I could almost see him with his dad's toolbox, installing the deadbolt on his bedroom door. Talk about a symbolic gesture. How many of us ever get the chance to lock away our old lives so we can reinvent ourselves from the ground up?

And what made it a really good story was that he had pulled it off! What a rush these weeks must have been for him—the house to himself, Didi in his arms! That old Jacob Garrett, Mathlete of the Year, must have seemed a million miles away.

And then everything fell apart.

I went to see Jake's lawyer, Mrs. Tidmarsh, and begged her to convince her client to come clean.

She was no help either. "Sorry, Rick. I work

for Jake and his dad. If they tell me that's what happened, I have to go with it."

"But it's bull! Jake's protecting this girl, and she's letting him take the fall! He's obsessed with her! Crazy, almost! He's unfit to stand trial!"

"I see you watch a lot of TV," she commented with a crooked smile.

"Let me be a witness," I suggested. "I'll tell the truth if Jake won't. I saw the whole thing."

"You want to help out Jake?" she asked seriously. "Fine. Go back to school and round up a bunch of his friends. On the morning of the hearing, you all get dressed up in your Sunday best and stand behind Jake so the judge sees that he's a nice all-American kid who's worth a second chance. I'll put a few of you up as character witnesses—things like that make a difference with a judge who has to look at gang members and juvenile delinquents all day."

So now I had a purpose. It wasn't the one I wanted, but as the guy said in that Dickens book, "The law is an ass"—although in this case it went more like "Jake Garrett is an ass when it comes to Didi, and that's why he's in trouble with the law."

Yes, it was stupid to have to defend a person with choirboy testimonials when you had genuine eyewitnesses to his innocence. But if that was the way I had to play it, I would.

I didn't expect to get anywhere with Didi, Jennifer, or Todd, and the partygoers from other schools would be impossible to track down. The Throckmorton Hall crowd had a different, but related, problem. After searching the Garrett house, the police discovered Jake's essay-writing operation, and turned over the evidence to Atlantica University. Now all of Jake's customers were facing expulsion, and even the people who were innocent didn't want to be associated with the scandal. As a source of character witnesses, A.U. was out.

That left just the Fitz kids, and they wouldn't be an easy sell either. Everybody's parents had read the newspaper accounts of the wild local party that had landed a two-hundred-sixty-pound lineman in the hospital, and very nearly burned a house to the ground. They now knew what their little darlings had been up to all these Friday nights.

My own folks had been running a miniature Spanish Inquisition ever since early Saturday morning when the nearby sirens had woken them up. And they *trusted* me. I had to assume that similar interrogations were going on all over town.

But Jake needed as many character witnesses as I could wheedle into showing up. I wasn't sure exactly who to approach at first, and finally decided there was strength in numbers. So I asked them all—everybody I knew, and everybody I recognized as having set foot in Jake's house. I wasn't pushy—I knew some people would feel that appearing on Jake's behalf was an act of disloyalty toward Todd and company. And anyway, Mrs. Tidmarsh didn't say she wanted to march an army into that courtroom.

I just spread the word about the time and the place, reminding everybody that Jake had shown us a lot of hospitality, and now he needed our help.

I talked Mr. DiPasquale, our assistant principal, into granting a half-day absence to anybody who wanted to go down to the courthouse. This was a school issue, I argued, since Fitzgerald High had made it one. They had canceled Saturday's football game, forcing the Broncos to forfeit. And they had suspended the team's long-snapper, pending the outcome of this hearing. I was encouraged to note that Mr. D. was doing a brisk business in passes.

"Just dress like it's the nineteen-fifties and you're in one of those lame TV shows," I advised people. "If we look wholesome, the judge is going to figure that Jake's wholesome too."

Following Jake's lawyer's advice, I fought down my instinct to argue the facts of the case, or to place blame. We were character witnesses, plain and simple. If someone copped an attitude, I backed right down. Jake's whole future was at stake here, and it wasn't going to help him if I ended up screaming at people.

For insurance, I put notices on every bulletin board in the building, reminders that we would be meeting on the east steps of the courthouse at eight-thirty sharp. I had one other thing working in my favor: at our school this year, Friday meant Jake. Only, this week, the party was a whole lot earlier, and I didn't think the judge would have a keg cooling in the witness box.

I went to bed Thursday night with a nervous knot in my stomach. But at least I had the satisfaction of knowing that I had done everything I could to help Jake.

Everything, that is, except tell the truth.

chapter
sixteen

FRIDAY WAS COLD and gloomy. I got to the courthouse at ten to eight, ridiculously early, I now saw. But I didn't want any of my character witnesses to show up and then leave, thinking they'd messed up the details or something. I'd appointed myself the standard-bearer, and I had to be there to rally the troops when they came.

It was a supremely uncomfortable vigil. It turned out I had outgrown my one suit, and could remain well dressed only if I didn't breathe too deeply. There I stood, choking on my tie, trying not to pop any buttons.

I started to get nervous around eight-fifteen. By eight-twenty-five, I was wound up so tight my suit was starting to fit. And I was still alone.

I descended the marble steps and looked up and down Eagle Street. There were people hurrying here and there, rushing to get to work. None of them were kids.

The eight-thirty bus lurched to a halt in front of the building. I held my breath as the doors opened. Surely half of Fitz would spill out on the sidewalk. One person exited. She looked to be about seventy.

I knew then. I should have known before. Nobody was coming to stand behind Jake. Not one solitary soul.

As the minutes ticked by, my tenseness morphed into an incredulous sickening despair. Mr. DiPasquale told me he'd given out sixty-three passes. Where were these people?

How could they be so heartless? So rotten? Were they that scared of what Todd thought? It didn't matter. For whatever reason, they weren't coming. Jake's house hadn't burned down last week. But everything he had built—his image, his status, his popularity—had gone up in smoke. He was unmade, not by fire, but by cold, smooth indifference.

Those bastards!

When eight-fifty rolled around, I headed up the stairs to take my place as Jake's one-man circle of friends. Maybe he was abandoned, but not by me.

"Hey, Rick—wait up!"

I wheeled. A pudgy figure in a rumpled suit that fit worse than mine was pounding up the courthouse steps. He looked kind of familiar, but I couldn't place him at first. Then a heavy footfall jarred loose a thickly-gelled cowlick, which sprang straight up on the crown of his head.

"Dipsy!" He couldn't have begun to fathom how overjoyed I was to see him.

"Sorry I'm late," he puffed. "My suit was in a box in the attic. Let's get in there and join the others."

"There are no others," I told him. "It's just us."

He gazed at me quizzically, like I was speaking a foreign language.

I spelled it out. "Not one single person showed up for Jake."

I knew exactly what he was feeling, because I felt it too.

He said, "They used to show up by the hundreds."

I was bitter. "Yeah, for free beer, free pizza, and free bedrooms. Not for Jake."

He nodded slowly. "The giant manta ray is

often seen with dozens of species surrounding its massive wingspan. But in the end, its fate is to prowl the oceans alone."

It was unfair to take out my anger and frustration on the only Fitzgerald student who didn't deserve it. But that was one fish story too many.

"What's your problem?" I snapped. "Every time something serious comes up, you disappear into 20,000 *Leagues Under the Sea!*"

"The remora—" he began.

"You're doing it again!" I practically howled. "Instead of answering me, you're talking about seafood!"

"But don't you remember?" he asked solemnly. "I'm a remora."

"What are you babbling about? What the hell is a remora anyway?"

"The remora is a small fish with a large suction cup on its back. It attaches itself to the bottom of a shark, just below the mouth. And it lives there, feeding off the bits and pieces of food that the shark misses." He smiled. "It's smaller than the shark, and weaker. But a shark never eats its remora."

I was suddenly blown away by what this kid was telling me about himself. It was nothing, yet it was *everything* about Dipsy. He had attached himself to Todd and his crowd in some kind of unspoken nonaggression pact—they let him hang around, and he put up with their jokes at his expense. And what was in it for Dipsy? He got to experience, albeit on the fringes, a social life that would have been barred to him as a pudgy, funny-looking junk-food addict who spoke in aquatic riddles. He got the scraps that fell from the careless jaws of the sharks.

"Is it worth it?" I asked in wonder.

He looked me straight in the eye. "I used to get picked on. *Really* picked on. Like, nobody's smiling when it's happening." The famous shrug. "This is better."

"To be their clown."

"To fit in the way that works right now," he said seriously. "Remember, a remora never graduates from the ocean. But next spring, I'm gone from high school."

I regarded him with a newfound respect. That was always the question with Dipsy—why? The answer was that, the whole time, Dipsy had known it was *temporary*.

We all had a handful of things we had to endure to get through this four-year ordeal known as high school—the abuse we absorbed, the butts we kissed, the opinions we choked back, the lies we ignored, the boredom we hid. All at once, I envied Dipsy the genius with which he had distilled the complex series of equations that defined his life at Fitz to this single axiom: he could make it, but he had to let a bunch of football players steal his pants. Maybe a similar simplification existed for the rest of us, if only we had the brains and the patience to sit down and work it out.

I put an arm around him. "Come on, remora. Let's go do this."

As we entered the courtroom, I tried to smooth down his cowlick. It popped right back up again.

The hearing was nothing like the courtroom dramas in movies or on TV. For starters, there were only eight of us there—Jake, Mr. Garrett, Mrs. Tidmarsh, the prosecutor, the judge, a court clerk, Dipsy and me.

To be honest, I didn't understand much of what was going on. It definitely wasn't a real trial. It seemed more like a trial over what kind of trial to have. At seventeen, Jake could be charged as an adult, but he could also be considered a juvenile in the eyes of the law. Jake's side was clearly hoping for the second option.

I did my best to catch Jake's attention, but he sat sandwiched between his father and his lawyer, eyes front. There was no trace of the Jake smile, or his usual jaunty confidence. He looked miserable. Worse, he looked defeated before this thing had even started.

For some reason, there were no arguments. The prosecutor didn't present Jake as a serial killer who specialized in champagne bottles, and Jake's lawyer didn't counter that her client was a saintly boy scout who was far too busy earning merit badges to commit any crime. Instead, they shuffled a lot of paper, passing documents back and forth. It reminded me of the way my mom had described a real-estate deal—a closing on a house. *Law and Order* it wasn't.

I tapped Mrs. Tidmarsh on the shoulder. "When do the character witnesses go on?"

She just shook her head and shushed me. I caught a confused shrug from Dipsy on the bench beside me.

I tried again. "What's next? Opening arguments?"

"No," she whispered. "Sentencing."

"*Sentencing?*" I must have screamed it, because the judge glared at me and raised his gavel like I was going to get it over the head.

Mrs. Tidmarsh tried to put a hand on my shoulder, and Dipsy grabbed the back of my jacket. But I was already on my feet, yelling at the judge.

"Sentencing? Are you crazy? You don't sentence a guy who didn't do it! It was Didi Ray, and this poor jerk thinks he's protecting her—"

That was as far as I got before a large bailiff ran in and frog-marched me out of the court. He pushed me into the men's room, and ordered me to splash cold water on my face.

"But I've got to get back in there!" I pleaded frantically.

"Not a chance, kid." And he threw me out of the building.

I was nearly nuts, close to tears and shaking. I pictured the judge sentencing Jake to jail time— and all because of Didi, who never gave a thought to anybody but herself.

Blinded by emotion, I threw the heavy doors open and rushed back into the courthouse. Yes, I'd promised Mrs. Tidmarsh I wouldn't interfere. But it seemed clear to me that she was a lousy lawyer. Either that or she was in on the conspiracy to railroad Jake.

They had to listen to me. Here, of all places,

surely the truth meant something.

I never made it back to the hearing. The bailiff was waiting for me. He grabbed me in a bear hug and held on.

"You look like a nice kid," he said without much conviction. "You don't want to make me arrest you."

Back out on the steps, I slumped down and huddled against the banister. Never in my life had I felt such a deep, all-pervading helplessness. People rushed past me, hurrying in and out of the building—court employees, jurors, police officers; I was even caught in the middle of a small wedding, and wound up covered in confetti. The world was carrying on at its usual breakneck pace for everybody except Jake. His life was coming to a grinding halt just inside those doors. Didi could have put a stop to it with a few words out of her exquisitely formed mouth. Instead, she wasn't even interested enough in the outcome to put in an appearance.

Out of all of them, only Dipsy had cared enough to show up—Dipsy, who they teased and tormented. Maybe there was something about being picked on that was character building, that made you a human being.

The old Jacob Garrett, the nerd from McKinley,

Didi's math tutor, had been no stranger to that kind of abuse. In creating his new self and placing it at the center of their world, he had beaten them at their own game. They were never going to forgive him for that.

"Hey, baby, what's wrong?"

I looked up, and Jake was standing there.

Jake! I thought I'd never see him again.

I jumped up, grabbed the guy by the shoulders, and shook him like a rag doll. "What happened? What are you doing here?"

"They gave me a suspended sentence," he explained. "It was part of the deal we made with the prosecutor. That's why nobody was testifying. It was all over before it started."

So many different emotions struck me at the same moment that I was torn to bits. I felt stupid for screaming at the judge, and even a little irritated that they'd let me go on believing Jake was in real jeopardy of going to jail. But mostly, a flood of cool relief washed over me. Jake was all right, and that single fact trumped any embarrassment or resentment on my end. Thank God!

I caught sight of Mrs. Tidmarsh—not such a bad lawyer after all—standing a few yards away with Jake's dad and Dipsy.

"That's *awesome*," I breathed shakily. "Congratulations, man! I was freaking out!"

"Thanks for coming, baby," he said sincerely. He paused. "Just you and Dipsy, huh? You didn't hear from anybody else, right? You know—Didi?"

I didn't even try to spare him. If anyone needed a dose of truth, straight up, it was Jake. "I begged her to come. She wouldn't."

He looked so devastated that I quickly added, "This is great news. You did it, Jake. You dodged the bullet."

He hesitated. "Not exactly—" His normally unflappable features seemed to collapse, like the face of a baby about to wail.

"What happened?"

"I have to leave." He was better, steadier, once it was out, as if, before, he had doubted his ability to say the words. "It was part of the deal. They don't prosecute, and I don't stay. I've got to go live with my mother."

I was stricken. It wasn't jail, but it *was* exile. Worse, it was Todd Buckley, winning again. But even as I felt hot anger suffusing my cheeks, I realized that this made a lot of sense. Jake couldn't exactly show up at school on Monday morning as if nothing had ever happened. He was done at Fitz.

I swallowed hard. "It's probably smart for you to get out of town for a while."

"Not for a while," he corrected. "For good. At least until I turn twenty-one, which is the same thing. By then, Didi . . ." His voice trailed off, the pain almost tangible.

I just stared at him, because there was nothing to say. It was a good thing he was going to Texas. Maybe from a distance, he'd be able to see that Didi wasn't worth his mindless devotion.

"When do you leave?" I asked finally.

"Tonight." From his pocket he produced a three-by-five index card and handed it to me. It had an address and telephone number in Houston.

"We'll keep in touch," I assured him. "We'll find a way."

He looked surprised. "Oh, right. Yeah, copy the number down for yourself before you give it to Didi."

He must have realized how insulting that sounded, because he suddenly became flustered. "You've been great, baby—the best! I—" He enfolded me in an awkward bear hug. But it wasn't an embrace of friendship. It was more like the desperate grasp of a drowning man.

I didn't know what to say. "They're crappy

people," I mumbled in his ear. "You're worth more than the lot of them put together."

Over his shoulder, I spotted a slender brunette in a trench coat hurrying down the marble steps. She caught my eye for a split second, and I recognized Jennifer. I hadn't seen her in the courtroom. Then again, I hadn't been in there very long before they kicked me out.

She took a tentative step in my direction. I turned away. I wasn't in the mood for Jennifer just then, and possibly ever.

Still, I was strangely glad she'd come. Jen the Merciless had a shred of conscience. Good for her.

She looked the other way as she rushed past us.

"Jake." Mr. Garrett's voice was gentle but firm. "You've got a lot of packing to do."

Jake stuck out his hand. "You've been a real friend, baby. I'll miss you."

We shook. "Take care, Jake."

I watched him say good-bye to Dipsy. Then he, his father, and his lawyer got into the Beamer, which was parked at the curb.

And Jake Garrett was whisked out of my life.

That night I saw my mother carrying a FOR SALE sign from the garage. I didn't have to ask her where it was going.

chapter
seventeen

FOOTBALL.

After all this, there was still football. Naturally, I quit the Broncos, but Coach Hammer didn't accept my resignation. He threatened to flunk me in Phys. Ed., which meant I wouldn't graduate that spring.

Rah, team.

Actually, there was one advantage to remaining a Bronco. When I ran up to kick that first field goal, there would be a delicious moment where even I wouldn't know what I'd be sending through the uprights—the ball, or Todd Buckley's lousy head.

The thought sustained me as I arrived at the field that Saturday. I clung to it, hugging it to my chest like a tiny perfect gem.

I was a little surprised to find the stands crowded, but strangely quiet. Then I realized what was missing. Dipsy—sparkplug, mascot, buffoon—was not in attendance today, screaming his lungs out as he gave his all to the Broncos and a two-pound bag of Doritos. Of course, it was early yet, but I really hoped he was staying away for good. Maybe I didn't have the guts to boycott this gang of backstabbers, but I loved the idea that the remora had relocated to another reef, where the sharks weren't so vicious.

In the locker room, the Broncos were trying to rev up some bloodlust without the natural gifts of Nelson Jaworski, who was out of danger, but still hospitalized. Nelson's dubious career in athletics—any athletics—was over. On the brighter side, he had reconciled with Melissa. His blow on the head had so scrambled his memory that he couldn't recall why he'd broken up with her in the first place. At least, that was my theory. Nelson wasn't the forgiving type.

The team mood was not very pleasant. No one was thrilled about last week's forfeit, and there wasn't much optimism about our prospects today. We were without our toughest lineman and our long-snapper.

"Damn that Garrett!" Todd spat, lacing his shoulder pads. "First he costs us Nelson. Then he costs us last week's game. Now he blows town, so we don't even have our long-snapper. And after all we did for him!"

"Yeah," I put in. "You even loaned him your girlfriend. Some gratitude."

I'd earned myself a punch in the face, and I was about to get one when Coach Hammer walked into the room, escorting a large man with a potbelly that extended halfway to infinity.

"Listen up, guys," barked the coach. "I want you to meet Sam Bloch from Eastern Illinois State. He's come to take in today's game. Let's show him what we've got."

It was the one thing that could divert Todd's mind from how much he wanted to deck me. When we took the field, Todd's famous front row would actually be host to a bona fide college scout! This was going to be the first day of the rest of his miserable self-centered life.

"Come here, Sam," Coach Hammer invited the guest. "Let me introduce you to Todd Buckley. You'll want to keep an eye on him."

"Sure," the big man said with a semi-interested shrug. "But where's this Garrett kid? I hear he'll give you a perfect long snap ninety-nine times out of a hundred. A guy like that will always have a place on a football team."

I glowed in the warmth of that statement all through the game. Glowing wasn't easy. We got killed, which was definitely justice. I had to hold myself back from cheering every blown snap. Remember, the back-up long-snapper should have been Nelson, so we were down to volunteers. Coach Hammer looked like he was ready to get out there and do the job himself. But nothing would have helped. The final score was 28–3.

I didn't mind because I didn't care. I walked out of the clubhouse as the only Bronco with a clear conscience.

Something smacked me in the back of the head, and I wheeled, expecting to face an angry Todd. But there was no one there. My teammates had all hung out for the postgame postmortem.

And then the next projectile was incoming, a crab apple aimed with deadly accuracy at the center of my forehead. I ducked, and it sizzled by my ear.

That was when I saw her, perched in the tree by the end of the sidewalk.

I wasn't in the mood for our usual games. "What are you doing, Jen?"

She hopped down to the ground. "Hey, Ricky. I just remembered. I owe you an apple-picking."

Apple-picking. Two years of silence on the subject, and now here it was, out in the open.

I picked up the first crab apple with every intention of winging it at her. Instead, I said, "Just because I play along with your Warrior Princess crap doesn't mean I don't have feelings."

"I have feelings too," she told me.

"Caffeine dependency isn't a feeling."

"That day in the orchard," she persisted with my favorite subject, "how do you think it made me feel when I heard you'd been making out with Hayley DeLuca the night before?"

I gawked at her. "I never touched Hayley DeLuca!"

"I figured that out," she snapped. "*Later*! But when Todd hit me with that story in the middle of a bunch of people, what was I supposed to think?" She looked at me earnestly. "It's enough to make a girl do something stupid."

I didn't know whether to be happy or furious. "Two years!" I exclaimed. "I thought you blew me off! Why didn't you tell me?"

"Would it have made any difference? It still happened. You know me, Ricky. I'm not a *then* person; I'm a *now* person. I only talk about the past when there's something big at stake. Like you and me."

You and me. I could hardly believe it. It had taken two years, but we'd finally reached a point where there was nothing at all standing in the way of *you and me.*

But first we had to clear the air.

"Your friends hate my guts."

She shrugged. "That's their problem. We've all got our faults. I don't give to Greenpeace." She looked down with a half shrug. "And I can be sort of kind of a bitch."

"I think Starbucks is a ripoff," I volunteered, adding, "but I'll still go there for your sake."

She squeezed my hand, disarming me of the crab apple. "I always knew you were a hopeless romantic, Ricky. That's why I never gave up on you."

I squeezed back. "I learned from the world champion."

She nodded sadly. "Jake. What's going to happen to him?"

I sighed. "He's going to be miserable for a long time. And then one day, he'll wake up, and go to his new school. And somewhere between algebra and a tuna-fish sandwich it'll dawn on him that the world didn't come to an end."

"I wonder if he'll be the new Jake or the old Jake there," she mused.

"There's only one Jake," I said firmly. Understatement of the century.

Still hand in hand, we began to walk away from the school.

"He did it all on purpose, right?" she asked after a moment. "Planned it out like one of his chess matches. Operation Didi or something."

"Guys have done more to get a girl," I pointed out.

"Yeah? Name one."

"That king from the Trojan War," I replied. "He sent a thousand ships to get Helen back."

Jennifer whistled. "Man, she must have had it going on."

"She was hot," I agreed. "But she was no Warrior Princess."